DRAGONTALES #14

SECRET OF THE SPHINX

by Rhondi Vilott

Illustrations by Freya Tanz

A SIGNET BOOK

NEW AMERICAN LIBRARY

Copyright © 1985 by Rhondi Vilott Salsitz

Illustrations copyright © 1985 by Freya Tanz

Cover art by Tom Hallman

DRAGONTALES is a trademark of New American Library

SIGNET, SIGNET CLASSIC, MENTOR, PLUME, MERIDIAN and NAL BOOKS
are published by New American Library,
1633 Broadway, New York, New York 10019

First Printing, June, 1985

    3   4   5   6   7   8   9

PRINTED IN THE UNITED STATES OF AMERICA

For Aaron, from your stepmummy

As you step out on deck, the ship pitches wildly, and a fine spray soaks you from head to foot. You shiver and wipe your face off, and belt the oversized tunic of your master tighter around the waist, its white fabric with the red cross bunching up, for though you're tall and stocky for your thirteen years, you have far to go before matching the size of Sir Hewbert the Broad!

Below deck you have been working on the knight's equipment, readying for landing, along with the other pages and squires of the crusading warriors, but the ship is confining and your stomach has protested this latest squall heartily. Fresh air has been your only comfort.

Still, it could be worse. The storm has kept Al-Hakim from sending ships out to meet you, and it looks as though you will be landing at the Coral Island fortress without too much trouble.

You crack your knuckles. Soon the Holy Lands will be safe again, and you will be made a knight by Sir Hewbert for your services! You can hardly wait.

Offshore somewhere, in the gray stormy distance, is the Nile Delta, and you shiver as you remember your Latin lessons and fables told of the Egyptian queen Cleopatra . . . and wild legends beyond that, which the friars would have thumped your knuckles for. But this is why you begged to be taken into service as a page and followed Sir Hewbert all the way from England. Adventure! Strange lands . . . and more.

You gulp as the ship rocks under your feet once more, and you grab for a hold on the rails.

Sir Hewbert drops a heavy hand on your shoulder, laughing loudly. "Is that a shirt or a nightdress, Matthew, my boy? You look a little peaked."

"One of your old tunics, sir, that you wanted me to make into rags. I hope you don't mind. The sea leaks have soaked my baggage, but I managed to keep your things dry."

Sir Hewbert smiles, his brown hair wild about his coarse-featured face, and his heavy fingers grip you so tightly that you know you will have bruises, mail shirt under the tunic or no. "Good lad. I see the armor master cut that down for you well enough. You have a way to go before you can match my girth! Here, take my short sword down and sharpen it a bit." He puts his sword through your wide belt, making you feel almost warriorlike.

You duck away from his affectionate cuff, but as you do, you slip on the wet decking, and the boat heaves again, and a massive spray washes toward the two of you. Sir Hewbert falls to his knees and clutches at a rope trailing from the rigging, as crewmen shout and scramble to save themselves. Your feet slip from under you, and you slide across on your back, as helpless as a turtle flipped upside down, your hands clawing madly for something, anything, to keep you from washing over the railing.

A metal object nailed into the wood deck snags you. It's that odd piece of bronze you noticed the day before, and an Italian sailor told you was there for good luck, with a shrug and an apologetic smile for his heavily accented Latin. An ankh, he called it, whatever that was. Whatever it is, you grab it for dear life, as the wave carries you with it and your feet dangle over the side of the boat. You sputter in the salt water.

The ankh is shaped almost like a cross, with its haft and crossbar, but the top piece is a curved oval, bent back on itself. It is that oval that is nailed to the deck, and your hands are wrapped firmly about the staff, but even as you struggle to pull yourself back onto better footing and to grab the railing or a rope, the ship rocks again.

Amid the cries of alarm from the seaman, you hear the rip of nails pulling free and—oh, no! The ankh comes off the deck and you are being thrown through the air, tumbling, turning, splashing into the ice-cold sea. You gulp and gasp for breath, as the water pulls you, dressed in the heavy mail coat and woolens, down to the bottom.

You awaken, shivering and sandy, the ankh still grasped in your hands, on silt-laden ground. The seawater patters gently about you as you sit up. You cough several times, for your chest aches, and you're aware that the storm is gone, as if it had never been, and the hot sun beats down on you, and the still air echoes with the cry of faraway birds. You've been washed ashore, but how, you don't know. By all rights you should be dead . . . sunk to the bottom of the sea like a rock, for you can't swim well, and in this oversized tunic and coat, not at all.

Your boots squish as you stand. A dizziness makes you sit down abruptly, and you hold your aching head in your hands. You can't remember how you got here, except that there was a gut-wrenching darkness just before you blacked out, and the ankh in your hands felt like fire. You look at the good-luck object as it winks in the sun. Made of bronze, probably, and a good two hands long in span. It's obviously not a weapon, but what it can be, you've no idea. You pick the ankh up and tuck it in your belt, along with the bared sword.

"You're good luck to me, anyway," you mutter. You stand up again. In this sun, you've no doubt you'll be dry shortly. You flip your hair out of your face. It's dark, almost black, and cut like the other pages', straight across the top in bangs, and straight at the shoulders. So common is the cut that barbers call it the pageboy. With a tug at your belt, you survey your surroundings . . . and see that you're standing at the flats of a great river, surrounded by reeds and grasses.

If you want to stay dry, you can't stay here. And if you want to catch up with Sir Hewbert and the crusaders, you had better find a boat or a trade caravan quickly.

With a crunch and a scrunch, you head out of the reeds, surprising marsh birds as you go. Suddenly, you are surrounded by bleatings and baas, as you walk right into a herd of grazing sheep, and their woolly bodies bounce in confusion.

A boy stands there, his staff in his hand, his dark eyes wide at your appearance. His skin is nearly brown, tanned by the sun, and his hair is black, clinging in soft black tufts to his skull, cut very short. His robe is long and of the purest white. Yours feels gray and dirty in comparison. The boy is tall and slim, and his eyes flash, as he closes his surprised mouth and abruptly swings the staff around so that he can use it as a weapon.

He calls out words that you can't understand, but you know a challenge when you hear one, and your hand drops automatically to the sword in your belt, but the ankh meets your fingers instead.

". . . or foe?" the boy finishes, and it's your turn for your mouth to open in astonishment, for suddenly you can understand him.

The staff remains in position, and the boy repeats, "Who are you and what are you doing with my flock? Cut their throats and I'll crack your skull open, stranger."

You spread your hands, wondering if you've been bewitched, and say, "I was swept overboard. . . ."

Your strange words cut the air, and the boy frowns as he strides closer, the sheep darting away in confusion. The staff cuts through the air at your temple, and you duck, grabbing for the ankh and saying, "All I want is a way out of here!"

The shepherd boy freezes as though he has understood everything you say. He points at you. "You carry the ankh! But you look and dress like a foreigner. How is this?"

Good-luck talisman or what? Your fingers burn,

but you're too surprised to toss the object away from you. Crossing yourself suspiciously, you pull the ankh from your belt and hold it up. "I—I don't know what this is, but it saved my life . . . and somehow, it makes us understand each other."

The shepherd drops to one knee and bows, saying, "Mysteries of the gods I will never understand, but you are welcome, stranger, and I, Ramses, will help you as much as I can."

He takes the ankh from your hand gently, then pulls a leather thong from his sandals and ties the ankh about your neck, tucking it under your tunic and mailcoat and undershirt, where it lies warmly next to your skin. "A gift from the gods should never be treated lightly."

Your head swims in the hot sun. Is it possible you've died and gone to perdition for your sins? This talk of gods makes your skin crawl. A lamb butts against your leg, making it buckle under you, and you sit down very suddenly. Ramses runs to get a sack and comes back, and the two of you share a meal of bread and cheese and a drink you don't recognize, except that it is cool and sweetened. Soon you feel much better.

Ramses listens gravely as you tell your story of how you came to be washed up at the mouth of the Nile, for the Nile it is, he has confirmed. When you finish, he shakes his head in bewilderment.

"I know nothing of any of this. I have never heard of a crusade or a Holy Land or even a Jerusalem. And this queen of Egypt—Cleopatra—I know nothing of her, either. But I am a shepherd boy and know little, barely how to read and not how to scribe, for that is the profession of a learned man. Perhaps you should go to my great-uncle, who is a sage, and takes his place in the bazaar, and he will tell you of what has happened, for I have no doubt the gods have moved you here."

A grimace tugs at the corners of your mouth. "I can't do that, Ramses. Everyone will know I am a stranger here."

"You could wear one of my robes over your clothes. No one will pay attention to two dusty boys, anyway. If we must ask the Pharaoh himself, we will get help for you!"

"Pharaoh?"

Ramses frowns in puzzlement. "Our ruler! He is related directly to the gods, and will surely know what troubles you, if my uncle doesn't."

Stranger and stranger. All this talk of gods and pharaohs has bothered you greatly, for your Christian upbringing strictly forbids such heresy. And suppose this Ramses knows you are confused and alone, and has plans to sell you into slavery or some such? Can you trust him? Though you can't deny that the ankh has powers

you don't understand, you don't know if you
should follow Ramses's idea. You feel well now
and can walk out of here, if you wish. A boat
would be a better idea . . . buy or steal one,
and put out to sea, and try to catch up with Sir
Hewbert and the others.

But a bazaar! Your palms fairly itch to see
more of the sights and sounds of this new land.
What might you be missing? And Ramses has
treated you more than fairly.

1. *If you decide to trust and go with Ramses,
turn to Pathway 6 (page 34).*

2. *If you leave Ramses and go on your own,
turn to Pathway 11 (page 60).*

PATHWAY
1

"**B**egging your pardon, sir," you answer tightly, "but that is too far for my widowed mother to let me go. I am sorry."

The clawlike hand releases your shoulder, and Ahmed snorts. "Perhaps when you grow older, boy, and want a taste of adventure. Well, then, I will be off." He flips a coin. "Enjoy a luxury on me, old man."

The sage catches the coin spinning through the air before it can touch the dusty street of the bazaar, and once more, you look keenly at his white-lensed eyes. Surely the man must be able to see!

Ramses lets out his breath in a grateful sigh. "Thank the gods you refused, Matthew! Ahmed is a thief and worse."

You nod, though confused by all that is happening, as you flex your bent legs. "What about this Sphinx? What is it?"

"A wise and terrible beast that lives in the deserts, near the great pyramids the Pharaoh Khufu built for his tomb and to the glory of the gods. It has wings upon a lion's body, and a human's face. It is said the one you seek has a woman's countenance and torso. That I do not know. When you seek it out with the ankh, remember that it loves to riddle. If you can answer its puzzle, it will not eat you, but will answer your own riddle."

A terrible quest! With a shudder, you think ruefully that you might have been better off joining Ahmed's caravan. "I don't know . . ."

Ramses says eagerly, "But you have the ankh, Matthew. Surely we will be protected!"

"I can't take you with me."

The shepherd boy's excitement fades as he asks, "But why not?"

"Well . . . I don't even know how the ankh works. Or if it does!"

"If Uncle says it does, it will." Ramses jumps to his feet. "Thank you, Uncle!"

"Bless you, Ramses, heart of my hearts. Take your friend to the edge of the village, and when you are alone, take the ankh, both of you, in your hands, and ask what you wish of it."

"But what'll happen?" you ask as you get up

17

stiffly, your face flushed in the heat and your clothes harsh from salt water.

"That is for the gods to know," the blind sage answers as he waves you on to your destiny.

You pull the ankh out from under your tunic and mail shirt, and Ramses grasps it as you do. You have shed his robes and eaten and drunk at his table while he explained to his mother that his uncle has sent him on a task. Now you are in the shade of the outmost buildings. All is quiet in the heat of the day, and you squint your eyes against the white-hot sands of this city. What do you say? You clear your throat as Ramses waits.

"Ankh, take us to—um—the Sphinx."

Darkness surrounds you, sucking the very breath from your lungs, and you recognize the gut-wrenching feeling from when you were swept overboard—the ankh is working! Out of reflex, you drop one hand to the hilt of Sir Hewbert's short sword, but grip the ankh so tightly with the other that your knuckles turn white. Ramses's lips are pressed together thinly and there is a pallor under his natural color, and you wonder if the ankh's method of travel is making him as ill as it is you. Then, *whomp*! You tumble to hot sands as the air booms and the darkness explodes with a flash of light.

That you don't remember, you think, as Ramses lets go of the ankh and it falls to its place upon your chest. An ear-splitting roar sends your heart pounding as the two of you whirl, and great shadows stretch across the sands . . . great triangular shadows, buildings of some kind.

A breath of wonder escapes you. You've never seen anything like this before! Far beyond it is a river, and a city hugs the banks on the other side.

"The city of the pharaohs," says Ramses in awe.

Behind you is the edge of the wilderness, with sharp hills and angles, and even as the two of you step out from the pyramid's shadow to look at it, the roar sounds again.

A great form hurls itself through the air, pouncing in front of you, tail lashing from side to side.

Ramses throws himself face first onto the ground and lies down, his slender form trembling in fear under his shepherd's robes. But you look the great beast in the eye, and its feline, almost womanish-looking face stares boldly back at you, baring fangs as you declare, "Ask me your riddle, for I have one for you!"

It works on the Sphinx, just as it used to work on the castle bullies. Sometimes the best defense is a great offense.

The creature settles back on its haunches. "Know you the penalty if you fail to answer me correctly?"

"I know it." Your right hand curls tightly

19

about the sword hilt. You'll be darned if you'll accept it lying down, though! But you're good at riddles, and besides, you think you've heard a little about this creature in your studies, legendary though it's supposed to be.

The beast snarls, then says slowly, as its great claws knead the golden sands, "What crawls on four legs in the morning, stands on two legs at noon, and walks on three legs at dusk?"

You can scarcely contain the wide grin that splits your face, for you know this riddle well! "You speak of the ages of man, Sphinx . . . crawling as a baby when new, walking on two legs in his prime, and hobbling on two legs and a cane near the end of his life!"

The Sphinx rears up, with a great hissing and clawing, but you stand firmly as its wings raise a cloud of dust. The disappointed beast finally settles down, and you reach down and haul Ramses to his feet by the scruff of his neck.

"A riddle that has defeated the best of men, and a mere cubling answers it in less time than it takes to blink an eye," the Sphinx mourns. "Very well . . . what can I answer you?"

"I was brought here by this ankh"—you flash it in the eyes of the beast—"and a wise man has told me it not only brought me across land, but through the ages. How do I get home?"

The Sphinx settles upon its haunches with a

purring sound. "Ahhh, now . . . that is the trick. Let me think upon it."

At that, the eyes of the beast close and it lies motionless upon the sand. You and Ramses stare at it for a moment when it becomes apparent that the Sphinx has gone to sleep or into a trance, for it neither moves nor seems to notice any longer that you are there.

Finally, itching with impatience, you whisper to Ramses, "How long can this take?"

The boy shrugs. "I don't know."

The shadow of the pyramid creeps along the sands, closer and closer to you, like the sundial of a clock. Finally the Sphinx takes a deep breath and opens its eyes. The slanted brown orbs recognize you slowly.

It smiles. "The gods brought you. I will tell you what you need to know only if you bring me an object—the Beard of the Pharaoh."

Ramses gasps. "The Beard is one of the symbols of the Pharaoh's right to rule—and is buried with him. Matthew, that's impossible."

"Not impossible," the Sphinx answers. "The object can be found with the aid of Isis or Set, or by trying to find it in the pyramid yourself. Three paths have you to get it."

You can feel anger flushing your face. "But I answered your riddle!"

"Yes . . . and if I send you back before the gods are done with you, I, too, will suffer. Therefore, I require an object of power and knowledge to protect both of us! Bring me the Beard and I will answer your riddle. Fail to bring me the Beard and there is nothing I can do anyway!" With that, the Sphinx uncurls its tail from its haunches and springs into the air, disappearing into the wilderness framing it.

Even as Ramses mutters, "Set, mighty warrior—" you are deciding what it is you will do.

1. *If you look for the Beard on your own, turn to Pathway 20 (page 98).*

2. *But if you choose the beautiful goddess Isis, go to Pathway 15 (page 75).*

3. *Or, if you choose the mighty warrior Set, find Pathway 7 (page 39).*

PATHWAY
2

Quickly, for the sand threatens to overwhelm both of you and the tiny oil lamp as well, you pull the ankh out and grasp it firmly.

"Ankh, help us!"

The lamp sputters out, leaving you in total darkness, but you can feel the warm bronze talisman in your hands. Your ears roar with the noise of the showering sand, then all is quiet.

A brilliant light flares out, and Anubis stands, the light coming from his staff. He holds his arm about the shoulder of a simply dressed man, and the two of you are walking across a chamber to them.

Ramses cries out, "Father!" and runs to grab him.

Anubis smiles gently and releases the man, and the two of you watch as they hug each other.

Only you seem to be aware that you are in a huge chamber, and a boat is at Anubis's back, a strange boat, with wings and monsters carved to the fore and aft, and the boat is filled with urns and covered jars. Only you seem to be aware that the white robe covering Ramses's father is stained with a dark rust color.

You feel odd, as though you have little weight or substance. You catch Anubis staring at you, and he gives a little nod.

"Yes, stranger, all is not well. You did not survive the sand trap, nor did Ramses, nor did Naton here survive the high priests. But the ankh has brought you safely to my judgment, and I will see you board the soulboat for the heavens, and your names will be safely written in the scrolls of the dead."

At that, you realize you are no longer hot nor cold nor thirsty, and as the two Egyptians board the boat and reach out their hands for you, you join them gladly.

THE END

PATHWAY
3

![knot divider]

Shouting a great battle cry that you have heard Sir Hewbert use, you rush the beetles, and the great one behind you falls flat to the ground as you duck from its reach.

Ramses exhorts you from above, crying out, "That's the way! Look out! Behind you! To the side! Get him!"

As you slash and crunch through the gigantic beetles, you think that you will never step on a cockroach again, for you can't stand the horrible noises the scarabs are making as they die.

You whirl, for the biggest beetle rears on its rear pairs of legs, waving at you, eyes spinning and jaws clacking. This fellow means business! You run him through twice, through the top half of the chitin and through the second half, and the creature tumbles to the ground, squalling and kicking.

It dies with a horrible buzz, but you don't have time to celebrate, for dozens of its brothers rip it apart and descend upon you.

It's clear there will be no winner here, and puzzling. It's becoming obvious to you that the beetles want you alive—for they are not harming you, but herding you.

A chill runs down your spine as you shout up to Ramses, "I think they want to capture me!"

"Then run, Matthew. Here!" And Ramses begins to undo his sash, to drop a rope to you.

"You're too light . . . you'll never hold me!" Then, in the shaft of sunlight, you see shadows on the walls behind him. "Look out!"

You must decide now whether to let the beetles capture you or turn the battle into a fight to the finish . . . even if you lose, and the beatles gnaw on your bones. You shake that thought. No, you'd rather flee . . . and even if the beetles on Ramses's level come after you, you can outrun them easily. Surely the ankh wouldn't let you get lost!

1. *If you flee, turn to Pathway 23 (page 112).*
2. *Find your fate in Pathway 21 (page 106) if you let the scarab beetles capture you.*

PATHWAY
4

You crash into the room like a clumsy idiot, the ivory doors slamming shut behind you with a *boom!* that is final. You turn and kick at them to be sure, but the doors aren't opening again—at least, not in that direction.

You weren't the only object that crashed. A gold-and-ebony coffin clattered to the floor as you bumped into it, and you dust yourself off, feeling a little squeamish. Suppose there is something in it? The lid is ajar, and cracked down the long side seam.

"Don't be stupid," you mutter to yourself. "Whatever is in that coffin is long since dead. This place is ancient, remember."

You cup the ankh, trying desperately to conserve its last flickers. The golden aura is but a shadow of its former glory. You hold it up, trying to see across the room as best you can.

The entire room is filled with coffins, the great huge rounded coffins that Egyptians seem to favor, all stacked on end. You can't tell that way if they're full or empty. But what you can tell is that there is a door on the opposite side, and that looks like the way out to you. Confidently, you stride across the chamber.

A moan stops you in your tracks. You look at the floor. It looks earthen, but the floor and ceiling and even the walls all through the pyramid have been varied, some dirt and some wood, some tiled and even some sand. There could be wood under this thin layer of dirt. It certainly groaned as you stepped on it.

You lean down, spreading your fingertips and pressing down carefully. If this is a wooden floor, you don't want to go crashing through it as you did through the last one!

Your knees buckle as you lean and look, and a wailing sound makes you look back, between your ankles.

The sight you see freezes your scream in your throat, even upside down, as a figure wrapped in gray rags shambles out of the opened coffin! It raises its mittened hands and totters toward you.

You bolt across the room and stumble across another coffin, which crashes to the floor, popping its top. A second rag-wrapped being falls out and promptly begins to get to its feet, deaf, blind, and dumb though it might be.

This time nothing halts your scream. You stagger around the room, bumping into coffins and desperately trying to right the domino-like fall of the wooden boxes. Without another thought for anything but your sanity, you turn and plunge at the exit door, kicking it open in front of you, scant inches ahead of the room of groping dead men.

Find Pathway 36 (page 160).

PATHWAY
5

You hold the ankh out. "Here, take it—you must get free now, if Set is coming back to get you."

The goddess inclines her head, saying, "Matthew, your heart is big, but your head is a little hasty. You must think again."

The ankh trembles in your hands, and your eyes mist as you think of stout Sir Hewbert, the only father figure and protector you ever had. But you are in training to become a knight! And this is surely the most knightly thing you could ever do . . . to offer your weapon to her use and yourself to her service.

You go down on your knee and say solemnly, "Please take my ankh, Lady Isis, and use its powers for your own, and use me as your champion, if I can help you."

The weight of her cool hand rests on your

dark hair a moment, and an electric thrill runs through your body. Surely you will never be the same again! The warmth of the ankh is taken from your hand.

Isis jumps to her feet triumphantly, as the dark coils about her hands dissolve. You and Ramses move back, for a brilliant aura surrounds her body as she holds the ankh upward.

"Not Set nor all his minions can defeat me now. Ra, Osiris, my brothers and sisters, hear me!"

The chamber stills, and then rumbles, and cracks open, dome falling aside to reveal the sky—but what a sky it is! You must be in the sky, a part of it, for the stars twirl about you like snowflakes on Midwinter's Day! The earth is so far below as not to be seen, and you stand, like Ramses and Isis, on a brilliant shield. You can feel neither heat nor cold, but a wind streams your hair from your face.

Ramses takes your arm in fear, gulping. "She has taken us to the heavens with her!"

You can see the chariots approach, some drawn by horses and some drawn by beasts you have never seen the like of before, each chariot driven by a god or goddess. Their faces are most likely not seeable, for they wear headdresses and masks of animals and birds. Only the beautiful Isis can you stand to look upon, and now her beauty is terrible to see, too.

She cries out to a warrior of great strength and beauty and with the headdress of an eagle, "Osiris! Avenge me! Set made a cunning trap and captured me in the pyramid of Khufu . . . but look what I have! The great ankh he threw through the heavens, to wander in time and space unknown, has come back to me!"

The god reins his chariot to a halt, three white horses pawing and snorting at the sapphire-blue sky.

"There are intruders here, fair sister. Two mortals who have no right to be here."

She spreads her arms. "Then send them back before you draw and quarter Set for me!"

You gasp, to hear such warlike words from her fair lips, but before you do more, a thunder-clap sends you tumbling from the shield and you are falling, falling, falling . . .

Into a dark sea of salt and brine, as Sir Hewbert cries, "Hang on, lad!"

THE END

PATHWAY
6

$\longleftarrow \sim \longrightarrow$

Hesitantly you nod, saying, "I'd like to see your uncle, Ramses. I've got to find a way back to Sir Hewbert!"

With you helping, it doesn't take long for the two of you to herd the sheep back to the edge of the village, where Ramses pens them up for the night. Sheep smell, you think, as you shrug in your uncomfortably warm clothes. Their scent lies on top of the hot air and is woven into the robe Ramses hands you to cover your tunic. Another robe is the last thing you want to wear, as you feel suffocated now, but it's best to hide who you are. As for your blue eyes, Ramses just shakes his head and asks you to look at the ground as much as possible.

The village gives way to twisted, crowded streets like nothing you've ever seen before. Everywhere the people are dressed in thin wraps, and some of the women look more undressed than dressed! Ramses has to tug on your hem to keep you moving as you stare in shock at these people, going about their business, their sleek black hair hanging to their shoulders, with headbands and headdresses decorated with odd animals. And the richly dressed folk wear glittering colors about their eyes, making them large and colorful. Fans of huge plumes are carried by their slaves, delicately stirring the hot, thick air of the bazaar as the Egyptians stroll through it.

Soon, in the shade of one of the open stalls, you come across an old man sitting, his white-gummed eyes staring blindly at the streets. Ramses kneels in front of him and takes one of his hands.

Your heart plunges in despair. Blind! The old man is just a blind man, and surely not the wise man Ramses has declared him to be. Why, the old uncle won't even know why you are different.

You look around, wondering if you even want to go through with this, but Ramses signals you to kneel too, and to avoid odd looks in the crowded street, you do so. At least you're out of the way. Slavery looks to be common here, and the last thing you want is to end up as a serf to some cruel landholder.

The old man reaches out and takes your hand

as Ramses says only, "I have brought a friend, Uncle. He has a problem."

A shock runs through your head as your fingers touch, but the old man holds on to you, smoothing out your palm. You can feel your whole body shaking as though you are fearful. Clenching your teeth, you don't speak but wait for the blind man to speak first.

"Your friend indeed has a problem, one even the mighty Pharaoh cannot unravel, nor can I."

The white-lensed eyes seem to look right through you as he raises his head, fine-boned and fine-featured. His skin is as dark as Ramses's but his hair is combed back and neatly pinned. With a shock, you wonder if he can see you when he adds, "You have come from faraway lands, and farther still through time itself. You carry a talisman of great power, for the gods have called you to help them."

"Gods? What gods?" you blurt out.

"Osiris and his sister Isis and perhaps even the great sun-god, Ra, himself. Across the miles and through the years your path has led."

"Years, Uncle? What do you mean?" asks Ramses eagerly.

The blind man turns his many-wrinkled face from yours toward the boy. "I mean, Ramses, that he does not live in our lifetime, nor even your children's children's lifetime. He comes from so far away that we can scarcely imagine it.

It is the voice of the talisman he wears that tells me all of this."

Your tongue feels like cotton in your throat. Lost in time! Now you know you must be dead and your soul sent to torment, for you can't believe what's happening to you! "H-how do I go home?"

The blind man lets go of your hand. "I cannot answer that. There is only one who can . . . and you must use the power of your talisman to seek it. Only the great and wild Sphinx can answer your riddle."

Ramses laughs sharply. "If it doesn't eat him first!"

As you sit there, huddled, a clawlike hand grasps at the shoulder of your robe.

"Old man! I need camel boys for my caravan. How about lending me your grandson and this bundle of rags?"

You look around to see a hawk-nosed man, his eyes blazing with cruelty, dressed from head to toe in robes, not Egyptian but clearly from the surrounding countryside. A trader, perhaps, for he speaks of his caravan. His mouth curls as he says, "You could use the money, and we would return the boys safely."

The sage shakes his head firmly and says in a peaceful voice, "Go on your way, Ahmed. My boys will stay with me."

"Wait!" you sputter. "Which way do you travel?"

As he answers, you realize in wild hope that he is headed toward the region you know as the Holy Land. How can the old blind man be right—how can you have been sent through time by an ankh?

Yet even as your head buzzes, you realize that the ankh has given you the power to speak and understand Ramses's language, and that is magical. Why not the other? And if that is so, then you have no choice but to find the Sphinx, to learn how you may travel back to Sir Hewbert and the crusade.

Ahmed's black eyes blaze. "What about it, boy? Travel with me?"

Ramses looks at you, a silent appeal written on his face. He fears Ahmed and seems to be warning you.

The caravan or this mysterious beast, the Sphinx. What will you do?

1. If you go with Ahmed and the caravan, find your fate in Pathway 14 (page 70).

2. But, if you decide to find the Sphinx, your destiny lies in Pathway 1 (page 16).

PATHWAY
7

"If Set is a mighty warrior," you say, grasping at Ramses's last words, "then I'll take him!" After all, you're a page in training to someday become a knight!

But Ramses gasps at your words and falls to the ground in terror, as a dark cloud grows at the base of the pyramid and the stone structure shakes and opens to the interior.

The darkness flows about you, sucking you inside, leaving Ramses behind, and the door shuts with a great *boom!* Your ears pop as you look around, wondering why Ramses was so frightened and upset by your choice.

The ankh is dangling from your hand and gives out a white glow that seems to drive back the inky cloud. You tuck it into your belt, thinking that even if the gods don't need to see in this place, you do.

A cruel laugh rings out, and you can see the figure of a powerful man just beyond the edge of the light. Tall, with mighty legs and calves, and a bared chest, but you gulp as you see the outline of his head. A demon! Surely the man must be a demon, for he has the head of a vicious doglike creature. Your blood turns chill in your veins as you now know why Ramses showed such fear. Even as your own religion has the devil, so must the Egyptians'!

You're in terrible danger now, and all by your own choice. Still, there may be a way out, if you don't let Set know that you've guessed just how terrible he must be and are still willing to be a pawn to his plans.

The shadows at the god's back separate, and you see strange beasts . . . animals that naturally wear the head of the beast Set wears, snarling and snapping at one another, and beings that look like bodies, all wrapped in gray and musty rags, moaning as they stumble about, dead and yet undead, and great snakes that hiss and roil about Set's feet.

The god beckons to you. "Come, boy. You pledged yourself to me, and I answered your summons. Give me the ankh and let's be on our way! Osiris and Horus await my might!" The hyena head tilts back as he laughs again.

The ankh! Set wants your magical ankh. You

touch it where it is tucked into your belt, wondering why he just doesn't take it from you, and decide it is because the ankh must be given freely. And if he wants it that badly . . .

"Send me home, Sir Set, and I will give it to you!"

Another laugh sends your heart pounding, as the god beckons in derision, answering, "That is not within my power, boy, as other gods oppose me. But give me the ankh and no one will stop us!"

"I will give you the ankh if you will help me find the Beard of the Pharaoh, because the Sphinx says then it will help me."

The god hesitates, and his minions grow restless behind him. Then Set responds. "Follow me then, and remember what you have pledged!"

As the being moves away, you follow after, noticing that the god stays carefully just out of range of the ankh's light, and his minions flee and shriek to stay out of each other's way, lest a ray of the light touch them.

The ankh, then, must be a force for good in this strange world of warring gods. You touch it and feel its comforting force. As you move into the corridors and shafts of the mystical pyramid, you try to decide what you will do.

That you can never stay with Set, or surrender the ankh to him, you know! No knight could be so ignoble as to deliberately help evil. No, somehow you must either trick or flee the terrible god, and escape whatever plans Set may have for you.

Set turns a corner, and you are momentarily cut off from him. A sharp *"Psssst!"* captures your attention, and you stop.

The passageway you've traveled thus far is littered with huge urns, big enough to hide a man, filled with all sorts of things—grain, perfume, oil, even gold. From behind one of them, a wizened face peers out, and a short, stumpy man follows it. A dwarf! You've seen one in the king's court, a jester.

But this dwarf is undeniably Egyptian, dressed as he is, with a blue-and-gold-striped headdress, and a staff, and skirted like all the rest. His short-cropped beard covers only his chin and wags as he talks. "I'm Bes, the god of good luck. Flee and I will help you."

"But—" you begin, as Set's roar interrupts you.

"Boy! Where are you?"

You are fearful of the god of darkness. Yet you feel a little heartened, knowing that the good gods have not abandoned you. Will you flee, or go with Set deeper into the pyramid, hoping to trick him and avoid pursuit?

1. *If you decide to trick the evil god, turn to Pathway 18 (page 90).*

2. *Your fate lies in Pathway 24 (page 117) if you flee.*

PATHWAY

8

"No offense, ah, Lady Bast," you say to the cat. "But I think maybe I'm better off on my own, after all. Cats and I don't get along too well." With that, before you see if you've made the goddess angry, you turn on your heel and plunge down one of the corridors.

You can tell that the cat is trailing after you. Its loud purr sends a rattle through the corridor, and though every time you look back all you can see is a slanted pair of eyes in the shadows, you grit your teeth.

As you search through the endless maze of corridors, you trip stones that shoot loaded spears at you, avoid one stone that drops from the ceiling with all the force of the ton it must weigh (the cat narrowly avoids that one, too), and run smack into a coffin standing on end that opens, revealing a body all wrapped in musty cloth that makes you sneeze once you get over gasping for breath from fright.

Finally, you stumble to a halt, tired and hungry. You remember some dried jerky in your belt pouch and pull it out, thankful for your habit of always carrying a little extra food around on you. The cat flows around a corner and eyes you. It hasn't spoken since you first met, and you're grateful for that, because it unnerved you a lot.

The beast sits down and stares.

"I'll bet you're hungry, too," you mumble. You break off several strings of the jerky. "This stuff is dry and chewy, but it's not too bad." You throw it to the animal and watch as it sniffs, then settles down to eat delicately.

As you chew the smoky and slightly sweet beef, you settle back against the wall. "You know, I don't know why I'm here or what anybody expects me to do. I just want to go home and be a knight. I've worked hard for Sir Hewbert, and he's promised to see me complete my training. Why, I might even get to be made a knight in the Holy Lands, and help win the crusade. Then this happens to me, and I don't even know why. The Sphinx won't help me unless I steal something called the Beard of the Pharaoh, and it's supposed to be somewhere inside this spooky place. And Ramses says the gods must have sent me, but that can't be, because I don't even believe in them."

The cat finishes her snack and straightens up, watching you with her slanted stare. As you stare back, you realize how really tired you are. You've probably been wandering around in here the better part of the day. You close your eyes several times, and then your head rocks back as your drowsiness takes over.

Suddenly, you are sound asleep. As you drift in your dreams, wishing for Sir Hewbert, you hear a silky voice.

"You may not believe in the gods, but the gods believe in you, and you have shown a kindness to me. Therefore, I, Bast, will send you home. The arcane ankh will stay with me, for it was your task to deliver it. Farewell."

You come awake with a jerk, finding yourself in the dark and stifling hold below the deck of the rocking ship. Your wet clothes have been stripped from you, and you're wrapped in a smelly old blanket, but you feel warm. As you lift your head, a bundle curled at your feet lifts its head too, and the ship's cat looks at you.

You twitch your nose. "So it was all a dream! I must have knocked my head against the deck and Sir Hewbert caught me."

The ship's cat looks at you haughtily from deep green eyes and gives a disdainful sneeze, then curls back up again at your feet, keeping both of you warm.

You hesitate, wondering if you should shoo it away or not, and if you recognize the slanted green stare.

THIS IS THE END OF YOUR ADVENTURE

PATHWAY
9

Y ou gulp, fearing to go back in time, remembering what the blind sage told you. Then you take a deep breath. "I am already lost from my master and my time, Sir Anubis. Will you really send me back if I help this boy?"

The being regards you, amber eyes glowing with thoughts you can never hope to read. Then he inclines his head solemnly. "You will be sent to your own time and place, boy, if you defeat the curse successfully."

"Then I'll do it!" You take your hand off the sword, still grateful that you have it. Anubis waves his hand, and you feel your eyes growing tired. Barely have you closed them before your body goes limp and you slump to the ground.

You awaken in the shadow of a great building. A waterskin is by your side, and you grab it and suck greedily at the cool wetness it holds. Not until your thirst is gone do you bother to look up at the shade covering you. It's an immense triangle of a building, cut from huge stones. You swallow in awe, looking at its towering sides. What on earth can this possibly be?

You can hear steps crunching on the sand, and you duck back into the shade, but too late, for a young man cautiously backs around the corner and stumbles into you.

You stifle your surprise, for Anubis had warned you, but scarcely can you believe it—for this boy is the exact duplicate of Ramses—his sun-bronzed skin, his fine features and black tufted hair, his slender frame covered by a white robe, his sandaled feet. The boy's cocoa eyes widen, and you grab his shoulder and cover his mouth quickly before he screams.

"I won't hurt you," you whisper to him.

The boy blinks, then nods to show he understands you. You can tell he's been running, because he is panting and shaking, and you know you haven't scared him that much. The young man looks at your garb, strange to him. Then he smiles fleetingly. "Are you here to help me? Did the gods send you?"

"In a way. I know you need help. What's wrong?"

"I am Ramses," the boy tells you, and you think it must be a common name, like John or

Charles in England. "You've got to help me find my father!"

"Is he lost?"

"No. The Pharaoh died during the night, and the high priests came to get my father, to bring him here and kill him. You see, he designed the pyramid, and knows all of its secrets, and the priests will kill him so that no one can find or hurt the Pharaoh when he is finally buried here, three months hence."

Your nose wrinkles. Three months! That's a long time to wait for a burial. But you don't need to worry about that dead body—Anubis's quest was to help the boy, and now you understand a little, because the pyramid was built to honor the gods and protect the Pharaoh, and Anubis must have been pleased by its building, since he wants to help the boy and his father.

"Where are the priests now?"

"At the necropolis—the city of the dead—readying the Pharaoh's body. The heart and brain and other organs are removed, then the body is soaked for many weeks to preserve it, as are the organs." Ramses shudders. "My father deserves such a burial, too . . . but they will murder him instead and let him rot, like a peasant."

"Nobody's going to kill anybody if I can help it. Are you sure they'll do it here?"

Ramses nods, his lips tight and pale. "I'm

pretty sure. In fact, he may already be inside, waiting for them . . . or they may bring him back with them when they return from attending the Pharaoh."

"What's it like inside?"

The boy's face loses its fear for just a moment and shines in wonder. "The pyramid is huge, with tunnels and shafts leading in many directions. Some are false and some are traps, and some lead to the chambers honoring the gods, where the Pharaoh's treasures will be laid. Some of the chambers are full already with gold and such, awaiting the Pharaoh's pleasure in his afterlife, as he rides the soulboat to the heavens. There are paintings and histories depicting the greatness of the Pharaoh and his love for the gods."

"Must be some place. Did you say traps?"

Ramses answers, "Many of them. Clever and dangerous . . . and there are other things, too."

"Well . . . as I see it, we can wait until the high priests show up and try to trap one or two of them, in exchange for your father, or we can go inside and see if he's already here. Can you guide us once inside?"

The Egyptian boy shudders and says only, "It will be very dangerous inside. Only the map my father drew shows all of the secrets, and the high priests will destroy that map when the Pharaoh is laid to rest."

"We may have to chance it," is all you answer, but your chest grows tight as a drum, and your heart pounds within it. Anubis plans to make you earn your way home!

1. *If you plan to trap the high priests, go to Pathway 39 (page 168).*
2. *But if you and Ramses decide to search the great pyramid, find Pathway 32 (page 149).*

PATHWAY
10

With a shout, you pull your sword and charge down the stairs at the mighty Set, ankh-light flashing and setting the blade of your sword into a fiery glow. The god stands in amazement as you lunge at him, and he barely blocks the first thrust with a spear of jet-black hardness.

"Run, Lady Isis," you grunt, as the god beats you back. You duck away and stab the sword under Set's guard.

The god cries in pain and anger as a red welt opens along his ribs and blood swells, but not a single drop hits the ground before the wound begins to seal.

You should have known you couldn't kill a god! You fall back as the hyena-headed being lunges at you. The blade catches the haft of the spear again, and rapidly you exchange blows, the dull thunder of them reminding you of practice at quarterstaffs . . . something you'd never been the best at, and you had tasted the rain of many blows before, but not now! The blood roars through your head and your heart pounds and you feel as quick as lightning, for the god can't touch you, no matter how he howls and cries in anger.

Oh for a real sword! you think, but no matter. This one of Sir Hewbert's is doing well enough, as you dart in and cut low, and the god staggers back, one leg hewed nearly in half behind the knee. Crippled, but not for long! A howl of anguish shatters the air of the chamber, and as you look over your shoulder, you see the goddess hasn't fled, though she has risen off her couch and is poised for flight at the foot of the stairs.

Set raises a hand and cries out, "Mighty Apep! Answer your master's summons and cut down this mortal flesh!" Before you can do more, the evil god disappears in a flash of smoke, a shattered spear marking the battle you gave him.

You lower your sword, wondering what is to happen now, as a low rumble sounds. The goddess walks softly to your side, touching your arm. She is barely your height, and as you turn to look into her dark eyes, the lids painted with blues and gold, you think that you have never seen any girl more beautiful.

"Who are you, mortal?"

A hot flush runs over your face, and the sword trembles in your suddenly tired hand as you lower the point to the floor. "I—uh—Matthew, your—um—highness."

Her skin is fair, and the blackness of her hair shines like coal upon her head. A faint perfume drifts from her presence, and you drink it in, wondering what the fragrance is, and knowing you're never likely to smell it again, for she is a goddess.

"You carry my ankh well, champion of Isis. Few men would have been so bold or brave against Set."

"I, ah, well, maybe I just didn't know any better," you mutter, angry with yourself for not being able to think of something wonderful to tell her. As the ground trembles below you, you remember Set's summons. "What is an Apep, and should we run while we can?"

The goddess smiles sadly. "No, it is better to face the creature here than in the tunnels. Apep is the mightiest serpent of all the world, from below the earth. Its coils ripple throughout all the lands, making them tremble, and the mountains shake."

"Great. And I'm supposed to face that?" Your newly won heroism flees in the face of her words. You change hands on the blade long enough to wipe off your sweaty palm and then grip it tighter. "I hate snakes!"

"Don't worry. Apep's size is limited by the size of this chamber . . . and you carry the ankh. You may summon another to help you if you wish, though only the Sphinx would dare to face Apep, as they are natural enemies . . . but the Sphinx is likely to attack you as well."

"I can call the Sphinx?"

The goddess nods, and her loveliness does something weird to the pit of your stomach. You clutch at your thoughts. The Sphinx owes you, admittedly, and you might be able to direct its fury at the serpent. On the other hand, you're not too keen about facing Apep with the sword.

A loud hissing fills the chamber, and the ground buckles under you. You stagger back to the staircase as the earthen floor crumbles and moves aside, and the scaled head of a gigantic serpent determinedly makes its way upward.

Coil after coil pushes up as the scaled creature blossoms from the earth. You catch your breath after a quick "Yipe!"—for the head of the creature alone is as big as a small bear. Slanted eyes narrow at you, and the long forked tongue moves in and out, as the being hisses angrily. Fangs curl the serpent's lips.

"Careful," Isis warns in your ear, as if you have to be warned!

You flex your fingers about the sword grip. You'd almost rather face the Sphinx than this!

1. If you summon the great Sphinx to aid you, turn to Pathway 30 (page 140).

2. But if you desire to face mighty Apep, find Pathway 38 (page 165).

PATHWAY
11

Y ou shake Ramses's hand, bewildering the shepherd with this unfamiliar gesture. "I am a stranger here, and in danger. You've helped enough. If I stay by the shore, I may be able to find a fisherman to take me out and help me find my ship. Here." And you draw the ankh out from your shirt to give to him.

Ramses shakes his head firmly. "No! It's a gift from the gods of Egypt. The ankh stands for eternal life, and it must be meant for you, Matthew." He pronounces your name badly. Disappointment shades his dark face. "I'm sorry you won't come speak to my uncle, but you know best. I can't leave my flock." He stands and points with the crook of his staff. "That way."

You take your leave of the boy, even younger than yourself, yet so solemn in his beliefs.

As you walk along the riverbank and to the shore, you notice how dry and rocky this new land is. There is no doubt that a river such as the Nile would be of major importance, for the land itself seems parched and baked dry.

Your own lips are as dry and cracked as the ground, as you seek shelter and curl up under an odd tree, with huge leaves split like feathers. You wish that you hadn't been so quick to leave Ramses behind, you think, as your eyes droop to sleep, for you are too exhausted to walk on.

A whip's crack stings you awake, and you leap to your feet. A bare-chested man, wearing a headdress of striped material, glowers down at you. Then he smiles tightly and gestures to another man behind him. All are dressed differently from you, bare-chested, with short white skirts, similar to those the wild men of Scotland wear, and sandals, lightly clad under the hot sun.

"Here's a hefty lad! Another slave to do the glorious work of the Pharaoh!"

Before you can fight, your wrists are bound, and you are shoved into line with a group of men, dirty and tanned by the sun, their sweat glistening. "What is it we're to do?" you mutter, as the line of slaves is tugged after the men who captured you.

The man looks at you grimly. "The Pharaoh

wants us to build a pyramid like the great ones of the ancient pharaohs . . . even if we die trying!"

Your heart sinks as you realize you've made a terrible mistake leaving Ramses behind and striking off in this strange land on your own.

THE END

PATHWAY
12

You hesitate, then tuck the Beard into your belt. "I'll take this with me, and the spear, but I'm not sure what I'm going to do with them! Fill your pockets, Ramses. You deserve to enable your family to live well." You do the same, thinking of the armor and war-horse you wish to buy, and, taking gold coins, of an investment in land or a title perhaps. A single carved scarab falls into your pouch with the rest, and you keep it as a momento.

Ramses takes only a little. "Tomb robbing is a terrible crime here. If I am even suspected of it, I will be killed. So a little gem here and a little one there—they will think I am a skillful pickpocket and let it go at that!"

The two of you climb out and after much tugging, manage to bring the wall back down over the passage, so that the room is sealed again . . . though you barely escape with your lives, for an avalanche of dirt and rock follows it! Coughing, you stagger into the main maze of tunnels.

You hold the ankh out, its light now much clearer. "Ankh, guide us to the exit . . . we want to go outside."

The pull on your arm is unmistakable, and as it grows stronger and stronger, the two of you break into a run, until suddenly you find yourself before an open window, with sunlight blazing in.

"Stop!" you screech, just before Ramses threatens to barrel into you, knocking you right out of the pyramid.

You stand on the ledge and look a long, long way down. Finally you sigh. "All we can do is jump."

Ramses pushes past you for a look. He gulps. "Jump?"

You nod firmly. "I'll go first."

"Don't leave me here all alone!"

"Then we'll have to go together!"

Bravely, the two of you link hands and take a running start and leap into midair.

The Latin words you utter on the way down would have made your teacher blush, and Ramses mutters a similar oath in his language as the dry wind whips past your ears.

Suddenly a screeching swoops above you, and

claws rake at your shoulders, grabbing the two of you and slowing you down to a gentle landing upon the sand. The Sphinx beats its wings and settles beside you, with a fierce smile.

"A long jump for mortals—or did you think you had sprouted wings?"

You shrug. "It was the only way out."

"Death is but one of many doors," says the beast enigmatically. "Have you come to complete our bargain?"

But before you can answer, a perfumed cloud wafts on the air, and you recognize the fragrance. The goddess blooms once more, and walks out to smile at you.

"You have the spear, I see, champion of the ankh."

"And more." You look at the two of them, one a ferocious man-eating beast, and the other a vision of loveliness. And yet . . . which has the greater soul to understand what a man is all about?

Isis holds out her slender hand, a little impatiently. "Give me the spear and return the ankh, and we will see about your going home."

The Sphinx wrinkles its nose, shakes its mane, and gives a little snort. It says nothing, but its golden eyes look deeply into yours. Suddenly, you think you know its secret.

"I have found treasures," you answer slowly,

"and more. Magical objects and powers of the gods."

"Then return them to me," Isis orders. "You have no right to them."

"Perhaps not," you murmur, deciding.

1. If you give the objects back to Isis, find Pathway 37 (page 163).

2. Turn to Pathway 40 (page 173) if you give the objects to the Sphinx.

PATHWAY
13

As Ramses hesitates, you wave your sword and plunge at the evil god, remembering what Sir Hewbert always told you about demons and dragons and such not standing to face good honest metal.

The evil god stops laughing, and raises a jet-black spear to cast at you, and from under the cover of his shadow, you see a human figure, bound and tied.

"My father!" shouts Ramses. "He has my father!"

But the man is still alive, you think, and you twist away from the spear, chopping downward at it with the sword.

With a shower of sparks that illuminates the whole cavern, the spear disintegrates! You feel the tingle of power like a shock through your whole arm. The Egyptian god steps back, and even though there is no human expression on the hyena face, you think perhaps you've surprised him.

You step foward and slash again, as the god raises a sword of his own. The minions of Set flee, as the corridor and ramp light up with the weapons' clash, and you blink, for the scene, as clearly lit as it is, seems misty and far away to you.

Dreamlike, Ramses runs to his father and pulls him to the side, away from the battling god and you.

Clash! Clang! With every parry and thrust, your sword sings and sends out a shower of light—and the scene gets mistier and mistier, and you feel more like a ghost than a human being.

The sea! You can smell the salt tang of the sea breeze, and hear the mournful cry of the gulls! It's as though you're being drawn back with every blow you strike to free Ramses and his father.

"Not yet," you cry to the unseen forces pulling you back. "Not yet!"

Will you have the chance to defeat the evil god and save Ramses in time? You stagger back as Set presses his advantage with the sword, and a swift cut nicks your arm.

The pain is real enough! Fire shoots through you as crimson wells out, and you bite your lip to keep from crying in pain. You lunge point first at the bare chest of the powerful warrior and pierce him through!

A terrible rumbling shrieks through the pyramid, as the god Set dissolves into inky nothingness and disappears.

At the same time, you feel that gut-wrenching darkness inside yourself, and know from the shocked expression on Ramses's face that you are disappearing.

"I'm all right," you cry out. "Run for your freedom!"

And the Egyptian boy and his father help each other through the pyramid, as all fades away to a misty fogginess and your ears ring. But you know you are going home, as you triumphantly return the sword to its place in your belt.

THIS IS THE END OF THIS ADVENTURE.

PATHWAY
14

"I need work," you answer boldly, standing up and shaking off the man's hand. You're not sure what camels are, but at least the caravan is heading in the right direction.

Ramses is more than sad as he stands, too, and listens as Ahmed gives you directions to the well outside the town where the caravan is assembling. You hesitate before leaving.

"Thank you for your wisdom, Uncle."

The blind man nods and answers cryptically, "You must do as you must do."

Ramses, however, is not so serene as you tell him goodbye. He clasps your hand firmly. "Ramses I am named, for proud pharaohs now dead and buried in the Valley of Kings, but I don't feel proud now, for I have failed you."

"You haven't failed me! Listen, the caravan is

going to a region I know of—and I plan to find my own people there."

"If what my uncle says is true, your people are not yet born, but you must follow your own path. May Ra guide your steps and your soulboat safely to the heavens."

With that, Ramses presses away a look of anguish and runs out of the street, leaving you behind. The blind man seems no longer to notice you, and you trail away quietly. The rest of the afternoon you spend dodging traffic in the crowded bazaar until it is time to seek out the caravan.

The well is surrounded by large beasts that bawl and jostle each other to drink, sounding and smelling like very large billy goats. They have long, lanky legs, huge humps on their backs, ropelike tails, and long, curving necks. Strange creatures, these, and they protest as their humps are covered with sacks and boxes of goods and they are bridled and led from the well.

Ahmed nods as you walk up and points. "Get a camel, boy. You will be in charge of three of the beasts, so see that you earn your keep! You will help the other drivers whenever they need it."

The beast, its lanky legs folded under it, turns a gentle-seeming face to you as you grab its rein. You tug, but the camel ignores you, chewing placidly, rubbery lips foaming a little. Its eyes are a soft brown and longer-lashed than any girl's, but what stubbornness! Only a goat or a donkey could compare!

Days later, you would cheerfully kick any camel that you meet, save that you have learned they kick—and spit—much faster than you can dodge. Your feet burn in the desert sand, and your body aches all over, and to top that off, you can tell that the caravan has turned off course. As you sit huddled by the campfire wondering how the desert can be so darn hot by day and cold by night, you're aware that your camel is snoozing at your back. Rosie, as you've named her, isn't so bad. But the other two you would gladly reduce to a few tough steaks! Your stomach rumbles as it reminds you that are you hungry indeed, so hungry you can't sleep like the other exhausted drivers.

So it is that you hear the second-in-command, Kalif, as he whispers to Ahmed, "I don't like it, Ahmed. Days out of our way, and what for? To lay a false trail so that we won't be caught robbing the tombs."

"It will be worth it, Kalif. We've done it once before. As for those others, slit their throats, feed the desert, and we'll be all the richer for it."

Slit their throats! That's your throat they're

talking about! You freeze, your eyes shut, as you listen to their plans.

"The Valley of Kings has other hazards, you know," Kalif hisses. "The curse!"

"Forget the curse! Dead is dead. Come on. This time tomorrow we'll be up to our asps in gold!"

You lie very still long after the whispering ceases. In the heat of the day, you can do nothing . . . but tomorrow night, when the robbing starts, perhaps you can flee! You will do your best to see that Rosie gets a light load so that you can ride her to freedom.

But the day is long and hard and your feet are dragging in your steps as the night falls. Ahmed gathers all of you together as you reach a rocky and mountainous range.

The drivers know what is coming when Ahmed tells them of his plan to rob a tomb. Only one or two of the young ones, like yourself, turn pale and shake in their sandals. They know they must help or face death . . . but one of them whispers under his breath, "The curse will kill us all anyway."

The camels are staked, and Ahmed passes out the light shovels and trowels and a few lamps all of you are to share. You follow the others down into the hilly sections, where caves and sealed doors into the red dust look like windows into another world.

Many holes give silent testimony to tombs that have already been stripped, but Ahmed lets out a cry of triumph when he finds one that is still sealed. He lightly trowels away the dirt and holds a lantern high.

"Here! Here!"

And before anyone can say or do anything else, he breaks the seal and rams the door inward.

Your ears scream at the silent noise, and you fall to your knees. A whiff of strange perfume floods the night air, and you can almost see the cloud released by Ahmed's action. A ghost voice proclaims, "To those who have disturbed the Pharaoh's journey, may Set and his minions gnaw on your bones. A curse on you forever."

The camel driver next to you cries out, "The curse! The curse!"

Now is your chance to get away. You had planned to flee, but Rosie is too far away. The ankh rattles on your chest, warm against your skin. The ankh has mysterious powers. Can you use it to save yourself?

1. *If you decide to flee, go to Pathway 29 (page 136).*

2. *But if you use the ankh to save yourself, turn to Pathway 19 (page 95).*

PATHWAY
15

With a shrug, you say, "Isis, I guess," while Ramses gives a crow of joy.

His dark eyes flash. "She's beautiful, Matthew, and the goddess of magic and goodness. Of all the gods, I like her best—she's sure to help us."

"Let's hope so." After all your studying in Latin, and the stories you've heard of the Roman goddesses and their troublemaking, you're not so sure. On the other hand, you don't know much about girls, anyway. You just get all tongue-tied when you're around them, and they giggle a lot at you, which just makes everything that much worse. When you're a knight, though . . .

"Matthew?" Ramses asks.

"Huh? Oh, right. Well, that way, I guess," and you point back to the pyramid, wondering just how you're going to find Isis and tell her you'll help her, and ask if she'll help you.

The two of you study the weathered pyramid. It looks impossible to get into without help of some kind, and you sigh.

"How do we let Isis know, if we can't get inside?"

Ramses shrugs, then points, his eyes wide, at your glowing ankh. "Look! Look at that!"

A golden aura emanates from the bronze talisman, growing until a sphere big enough to hold a person separates, and floats gently to the ground. Inside, a white crystal shape unfolds, blossoms, and stretches into a lithe, beautiful figure hugged close by her pleated white gown. Kohl and precious colors decorate her eyelids, and her mouth is as red as if she had just eaten cherries. Her skin is untouched by the sun, and her features fine-boned. Her raven-black hair hangs to her shoulders, and upon her brow rests a circlet depicting a heron in flight. She smiles as Ramses falls face forward to the ground, and you go to one knee in awe.

"My name was called in distress, and I answered," says Isis as she comes forth from the golden sphere and it falls to shards about her on the sands, an eggshell that delivered a goddess.

She holds out a slender hand to you and helps you to stand. Ramses jumps up, dusting off his robes, stammering, "M-m-mighty Isis!"

Her laughter is as fresh to your ears as the sound of rain falling to the desert, you think, and then a hot flush runs over your face. You clear your throat and straighten your tunic, as she asks, "Which of you needs my aid?"

"I do," you answer, since Ramses seems unable to get a word out without strangling on it. "I need the Beard of the Pharaoh, and the Sphinx told me if I helped you, you might help me."

"Indeed." Her wide brown eyes regard you. You feel as though she can see all the way to your soul and beyond. Never before would you have thought there were really gods and goddesses outside your religion, but you are shaken to the very bottom of your boots. "How can I refuse you, when you carry one of the great ankhs? When you are finished here, I ask only that you leave me the talisman, for it bears great power."

"Here, then, take it," Ramses blurts out as he grabs the ankh from your hand and shoves it at the lady.

She frowns and shakes her head. "Never taken . . . only freely given. That is how the ankh must travel. Besides, the two of you will need it to complete the task I will give to you, in return for the Pharaoh's Beard. Bring me the jet spear of Set."

Ramses sucks in his breath, and the woman looks at him. "Never fear . . . Set does not carry it at the moment. It is at rest within the pyramid. As you know, I cannot touch it, but mortals may." She claps her hand, and an opening blossoms above you, and the wind blows furiously, and when it finishes, a ramp of sand leads to the doorway. "I will search out the Beard, and you will go for the spear. Let the ankh be your guide."

At that, she mounts the ramp and disappears.

Ramses hands you back the ankh, ashamed, his eyes not meeting yours. You clap him on the shoulder. "Forget it. A lady that beautiful would make anybody do crazy things."

The shepherd boy shudders. "You're not kidding. Matthew, Set is rarely far from his spear . . . it's one of his major weapons. He's evil, Set is, and dangerous."

"We have to trust Isis that we're going to be able to get that for her." You hold the ankh out. Its golden aura has not faded, and it pulls you, faintly but distinctly, up the ramp. Ramses trails after you.

Inside, the pyramid is close and still, its thick stone walls cool despite the blazing desert heat. The plastered walls contain pictures of the Pharaoh's life in every detail, and for a moment you are stunned by the exotic artwork. Then Ramses sneezes and the moment is lost, as the ankh pulls you ever downward and inward.

You can't shake off the idea that you're being

watched, and that something is following you, for there is a noise you can almost but not quite hear. As if reading your thoughts, Ramses whispers, "The pyramid is said to be filled with deathtraps and monsters to trap the unwary. The Pharaoh built it to the glory of the gods, and they promised to protect his body always."

"Do you hear that?" you answer as something scrabbles over the stone behind you.

"Almost, but—" Your friend shrugs. "We must be imagining things."

The ankh leads you around a sharp corner and straight down, its light sending you into a well. From far above, a golden shaft of light answers. Ramses points.

"Look! From the top of the pyramid—sunlight! There must be a window, high, high up . . . and when the sun reaches it, a shaft of light can be seen."

You stick the ankh in your belt, pull your sword, and descend into the well, leaving Ramses behind. He doesn't argue as you go alone, climbing handhold and toehold to the bottom. A second ramp leads into the shadows.

The walls are painted here, too, and the clay gleams in the sunlight, which is becoming fainter. You can see a pair of doors ahead of you, and a great seal is across their seam. You can't read it, but guess that a room or corridor of importance is ahead of you. You point the sword tip at the door, but hesitate to break it.

The scrabbling gets loud, and Ramses screams, "Look out!" as cracks in the walls literally burst with gigantic beetles. They are pouring down the well from all sides, chittering, their many legs waving, jet-dark in the shadows, as big as wild bears.

You jump back, pulling your sword, as they approach, their mandibles clacking and extra legs waving, backing you to the unknown ramp. The shaft of sunlight strikes you from above, and they hesitate a moment.

"Fight!" shouts Ramses. "Matthew!"

You lop off a leg, and the scarab beetle drops under the weight of its brothers trampling it to death. You shudder.

Golden ankh-light floods the well, and you guess that it has powers you can scarcely wonder at. The beetles are about to overwhelm you, and as Ramses gasps at something behind you, you can hear the clack of beetle jaws behind you as well!

1. *If you fight, turn to Pathway 3 (page 26).*
2. *But go to Pathway 27 (page 129) if you use your ankh against the giant beetles.*

PATHWAY
16

Y ou tumble inward, smacking your elbow and dropping everything. The ankh and the sword you gather up quickly, but you are in twilight, for only the talisman can pierce the cloak of darkness about the room.

You pull back, hitting the bronze doors, which are shut solidly. They ring out as though you had hit a gong.

The chittering and scrabbling noise that is aroused by the gong raises the hair on the back of your neck as you ready your sword. This is the last room in the world where you want to be!

Giant scarab beetles rise out of the dimness, their huge eyes glowing as their hairy legs wave at you and you cut and slash at them. Chips of beetle armor fly and joints fall twitching on the floor as you cut a swath through them.

You gag as you squish and crunch over their bodies. One of them latches onto the corner of your tunic, even though its head is completely detached from the rest of it. You bat and flinch at the creature as gore splatters, and finally it lets go and drops behind you.

The only thing that keeps you going is the sight of another door at the far end. The bronze doors that let you in will never let you out, but there might yet be an exit.

Ankh-light flickers on the dark wood ahead of you. You take a deep breath and ram the door with your shoulder. It bows along the seam but nothing happens.

The clacking and chittering grow intense behind you. You swallow, and with utter determination born of desperation, you throw yourself on the door, willing it to spill open!

Turn to Pathway 31 (page 145).

PATHWAY
17

With a deep breath, you twist your torso to free yourself and rip a length from your tunic. You tie one end to the ankh and, holding the other firmly, throw the talisman through the air, praying that the oval head will catch on the lever.

The oil lamp sputters as the mounding sands threaten to suffocate it as well as the two of you. Ramses's face is pale and his eyes wide with fright as only his head and the hand holding the lamp up remain free.

The ankh catches, and quickly you pull down with all your might. The lever slides down with a snap, and suddenly—*whoosh!*—the floor drops out from under you, sand and all!

You and Ramses catch each other as the sand falls away through grates in the floor. He is

shaking, and grasps the oil lamp with both hands, trying to still the quivering flame.

"You weren't kidding when you said this place has dangerous traps," you tell the boy.

He can only nod in response.

"Well, which way?"

Ramses takes a quavering breath to say, "I don't know. I mean . . . I'm not sure. We fell a ways . . . I don't know what level we're on."

You cast about and see at least three shafts leading from the room, now that the sand is gone and the lever has opened the doors. "Pick one, then."

Ramses shakes his head, too afraid of making a mistake. You look upward and see the ankh sliding down the lever and catch it, sash and all, as it plunges downward to you.

"Then I'll let the ankh decide," you tell the boy. You hold it loosely in your hands. "Point the way out." The bronze talisman tugs firmly toward the farthest door, and you step out, Ramses in your wake.

The shaft leads upward, growing narrower and narrower until you and Ramses must crawl. The boy gasps as he bumps into you from behind.

"I think we have found a dead end."

"No! There's a hole up here."

"Then be very careful . . . it could be a drop after you crawl through."

Heeding Ramses's words, you pause at the hole and reach back for the clay lamp. Ramses wiggles up next to you as you push the lamp through the hole, and the two of you peer down.

"Father!"

The pale orange light reflects a man, bound hand and foot, lying in a chamber. The room is brightly painted with animals and the river Nile, and figures of Egyptians. The man twists around, looking up.

"Ramses! What are you doing here?"

"We've come to save you," the boy says. He pushes ahead of you and wriggles through the hole, unafraid, to drop to the chamber floor.

As you land beside him, he is busy untying his father. The two hug each other tightly.

"And who is this?"

Ramses stops as he looks at you. "I—I don't know his name, Father. The gods sent him to help me."

"Then I thank you," the Egyptian says gravely as he takes your hand. "I am Naton."

"Call me Matthew," you answer. "Can you get us out of here?"

"Yes, but we must hurry."

"No fear of that!"

Guiding you through the twists and turns of the pyramid, Naton says little more, but holds the hand of his son gratefully, and you feel proud of yourself. You also feel the awe and the power of this immense structure created by this proud man.

Outside, the sun is dipping low over the sands as you step out on the ramp leading inward once more, and you realize you have been inside the pyramid the better part of a day.

You hesitate. Naton hugs Ramses close to him and says, "Now we must prepare to flee, son, for the high priests will never let me be. Will you come with us, stranger?"

You are reluctant to leave the building. "I—ah—I don't think so. I have other plans." You press the ankh into Ramses's hand. "Good luck go with you . . . and in case you're curious, Ramses is a very popular name for pharaohs."

The boy blushes and stammers his thank-you, and then the two of them hurry off across the sands.

There is a sound behind you, and Anubis moves out of the shadows of the now quiet pyramid.

"Good work, stranger. You fulfilled your promise, and now I shall keep mine. Close your eyes. . . ."

"Matthew! Get up, my lad! Anyone would think you'd drowned! Let go of that line and get yourself below deck!"

You open your eyes to a crusty and sputtering and very wet Sir Hewbert, and much to his surprise, you give him a great big hug.

THE END

PATHWAY
18

A‌s Set roars in anger, you hurry to catch up, and the golden light of the ankh drives his evil minions away from you when you turn the corner.

You bow. "I'm sorry, Sir Set, but I—I had a vision, and it stopped me right there in the corridor."

"A vision?" says the puzzled god.

"Yes! In the—ah—uppermost chambers of the pyramid, another ankh is hidden! This one draws me to it. If you would truly be all-powerful, you must possess both!"

The god puts his hands on his hips, considering your words. "The power of the ankh is limited until recharged, and from the light, I can tell yours is weakening! Yes, I have need of the second ankh. We will travel to the upper chambers. Be quick, boy, and stay close to me, for this pyramid is full of deathtraps for mortals!"

With a cruel laugh, Set turns on his heels and races down the corridor, his minions directly behind him.

A wizened hand plucks at your sleeve and draws you the other way, even as Set races after your false vision.

Bes smiles at you. "Well played, boy. The god of evil would never guess that a mortal man dared to cheat him."

"Who sent you?"

The dwarf bows. "Goddess Isis, beautiful lady that she is, the goddess of magic and goodness. It is her ankh that you carry, and she needs it back desperately. I will guide you as well as I am able to her side, and pray for both of us that Set does not find her first!"

You scurry after the quick-footed dwarf. "Do they fight?"

"Indeed they do! Isis is one of Set's most powerful rivals. But my lady has always managed to keep her power until recently, when the ankh was lost, thrown to a time and place unknown. You have brought it back!"

"Well, it's not going to do anybody much good if it runs out of power." You pant, as the dwarf leads you through a maze of shafts and corridors, some of cold stone, and some plastered, with colorful drawings and pictographs decorating their sides. Columns carved like the stems of leaves and flowers hold up some passageways, while others are filled with treasure. Still others echo silently with your steps.

Bes points down a corridor. "She is that way. I must leave you now, for another calls me. Beware the pit!" With that, the dwarf hops and disappears into the darkness.

The corner of your mouth twitches as you are reminded that luck is a fickle being in any land. You move forward cautiously so that the ring of ankh-light is always illuminating the forward passage.

A hissing and slithering fills the corridor. You shudder, for you're more afraid of snakes than just about anything. The light falls suddenly in front of you, into a deep pit, full of undulating bodies.

A pit of deadly snakes! You plunge to a halt, unable to go down the corridor any farther. As you take stock of the situation, you rest your hand against a decorated column, this time holding up a roof painted like the heavens. As you look at the column, you suddenly notice that the vine is real—not carved! It grows along the ceiling and down to the other side.

You pull the end of the vine off the column and tug on it. It's as securely fastened as a rope, and with a deep breath, you take a running leap and push up, swinging on the vine across the pit, as the snakes rouse and hiss ferociously, the ankh-light sweeping them.

You let go and land easily on the other side, as the vine trails back and hangs limply over the snake pit. You wipe the sweat from your forehead and wait for your heart to stop pounding. After this, you won't be afraid of anything, except maybe Sir Hewbert's temper!

You can hear voices from the corridor beyond. You move forward cautiously and find yourself on the top platform of steps leading down to a huge chamber, decorated with chariots and statues, and a couch of turquoise and gold upon which rests a beautiful woman.

Her hair is long and straight and combed from her brow by a coronet of gold, the front decorated with the graceful neck and head of a swan. Her gown of pleated white linen barely hides her beautiful form, and you gulp. You would be taken by her beauty, except that she is in danger, for the evil god Set stands in the chamber and is shouting at her!

"Give in, Isis! I have won this time!"

The beautiful lady shakes her head. "No. Stand back, I warn you, for even without my ankh, I have powers, Set, and you have tasted defeat by them before! Leave me now, before I summon Osiris and Ra and your body is once more scattered in the heavens!"

The hyena head roars with cruel amusement. "How sweetly you threaten me! You are powerless, for the ankh is weakening . . . I have seen it! A boy carries it, but he doesn't know what he has . . . and he has sent me on the trail of a second of the seven great ankhs."

You can't leave Isis to Set! Somehow, you must rescue her, but you hesitate. After all, you're only a boy . . . and these are supposed to be gods. On the other hand, you have her greatest weapon, even if it is weakening.

And you have Sir Hewbert's sword. As he has often told you, many a demon will flee at the touch of cold steel.

But which shall you choose? You know nothing of magic, and you have a long way to go in your knight's training.

1. If you choose to use the ankh, turn to Pathway 43 (page 180).

2. Go to Pathway 10 (page 54) if you use your sword.

PATHWAY
19

Y ou yank out the ankh and grab it fiercely in your left hand as you back away. The air is full of howls and wraithlike figures, and the tomb robbers about you are crying in terror.

"Do your stuff, ankh," you mutter, wondering if this will work at all, as Ahmed kicks aside Kalif and plunges ahead into the darkened tomb anyway, his oil lamp leaving a streak of orange smoke behind him.

A shriek of anguish pierces the air, rising and falling, then cuts away quickly as though it had never been. The tomb is silent.

Then all eyes turn to the mouth of the tomb. Heads raise slowly, faces etched in fear but looking in spite of themselves, as though bid. You, too, look, as the ankh turns warm in your hands.

The dark cloud issuing from the mouth of the tomb rises into the sky, a black stain upon the Egyptian night. In its midst, you see a towering figure, a demon you think, a man with the head of a terrible beast. He wears the pleated white skirt that you saw worn by nobles in Ramses's city, and his broad chest is bare. Wristbands of jewels and leather adorn his powerful arms, and as he throws his head back and laughs at you, shivers go down your back.

The tomb robbers press their faces into the dirt, crying, "Set! Set!" and huddle, trying not to be seen by the terrible eyes of their god of evil and darkness.

You gulp, for the being has seen only one— and that one is you. Even though your feet are glued to the ground, the ankh moves in your hands, dragging you to the feet of the Egyptian god.

The beast headdress moves in a grimace which you suppose must be a smile. "My thanks, underling. You have brought this back to me from another time and place. For that you will be richly rewarded. Now . . . what would you like? The form of an asp, second only to the great serpent Apep? Perhaps a crocodile . . . or maybe . . ."

Your head spins and your knees weaken, as

you realize that the god's reward is to send you into the body of a horrible beast, to serve him for all eternity.

THE END

PATHWAY
20

$$\vdash\!\!\!\sim\!\!\!\dashv$$

You take Ramses's arm in disgust, saying, "I don't see any reason to trust any of these so-called gods. We can find that Beard on our own."

As Ramses squeaks, "We can?" you pull him out of the brilliant sunlight and back into the shade of the pyramid. The shepherd boy watches as you stalk around the ancient building, trying to figure out a way in.

The two of you stop, brows furrowed, and you cross your arms. "There is a way in here, isn't there?"

"Oh, yes—but it's hidden! Only the high priests know of it." Ramses's voice trails off as he adds, "I can't believe I'm here."

The blocks are so neatly fitted together that you couldn't even slip the blade of the sword into the cracks between them. As you frown, you suddenly spot what must have been an earthen ramp and is not just a pile-up of sand and dirt from the wind. You walk over to the ramp. "There it is!" Above you, you can clearly see what must be a door outlined in the blocks.

You turn quickly to Ramses. "Let me stand on your shoulders!"

"B-but . . . ." the boy stammers, then braces himself. "Matthew, you can't go in there! There are traps and dead ends and . . . and monsters, all set to keep the tomb from being intruded upon. Why, I've heard there are levels and levels and only one holds the true burial chamber . . . and that's where you've got to go to get the Pharaoh's Beard!"

"Don't be so cheerful about the whole thing," you grunt in return, as you climb upon the slender boy's shoulders. He's stronger than he looks, for he holds you steady as you pull yourself up on a tiny ledge and use the hilt of the sword to knock upon the blocks.

Suddenly, with a grinding noise and a stale smell, a block moves, and a black mouth of an entrance leads into the pyramid! You crawl inside, turn around, and lean over to look down on Ramses.

"I'll lower my belt and pull you up," you call to your friend, who is massaging his shoulders ruefully.

After a lot of wiggling, you decide it'll be

easier to stand up, take off your belt, and then lie down to pull him up, so you do. But as you tug on the leather strap, suddenly the stone under your feet moves and dumps you backward—into the pyramid—and the door stone snaps shut!

You pound on the stone as you search frantically for the keystone that opened the door, but you can't find anything. The darkness of the interior of the pyramid stifles you, and you stop, sobbing for breath, your fingertips torn and dirtied.

After a long minute, just when you decide you've been buried alive, you feel the warmth inside your shirt. As you look down, you can see the glow, even through the layers of cloth and the mail coat. As you pull it out, the ankh is glowing like a tiny sun, throwing out a brilliant white light.

"Well, at least I've got you," you mutter, as you tuck it into your belt and remove the sword, just in case you need it. You're not sure what kind of monsters might roam the pyramid, or how they'd stay alive to do it, but you don't want to find out without Sir Hewbert's trusty weapon ready.

The light now shows you the bare outline of the door, and a seal inscribed at about shoulder height to you. You've no doubt that if you push it, the door will open. Then again, Ramses has told you there are traps inside Khufu's pyramid. You decide to wait until you've found the Beard and then see if the ankh's magic can help you get out. Ramses will just have to wait outside until you get back.

As you walk into the depths of the pyramid, you notice the brilliant paintings on the reddish clay walls. The stone has been smoothly plastered over to give the artists a surface to decorate, and the many strange symbols and pictures draw your eye. Though the ankh has given you the power to speak and understand, you can barely read your own language, and this one is incomprehensible, though it speaks in pictures as well as symbols. But the paintings above it are explanatory. Over and over again, one man stands out as a giant . . . and as some of the paintings show him in a chariot as a warrior, or in a boat fighting strange beasts in the water, you decide that must be the Pharaoh himself. You wonder if he was really that much bigger than everybody else.

Suddenly, the corridor twists and shoots downward so sharply that you scramble for balance. As you do, you toe a piece of stone sticking out at the bottom.

With a *whoosh!* of air that pops your ears, the passageway drops completely from under you and you tumble down with it, landing with an

101

oof and thump on hard sand. The ankh lands under you, and for a moment you're in total darkness, with the bronze object bruising your hip. As you dig it out for light, a monstrous figure looms at you, and you let out a yelp of surprise.

Ebony and white, the being glares at you, spear in hand, like a demon straight out of hell. Your heart pounds as you lurch to your feet and prepare to run. Then you realize you're facing a statue!

You hold the ankh up. The statue has the head of a hawk and the body of a powerful man. He's dressed for war, and gold shines next to the ebony paint, decorating powerful muscles. You swallow as you lower the sword in your right hand. The only thing this fellow is good for is a good scare—and he just gave you one!

As you twist around, you can see several corridors leading off, including a door hidden behind the body of the statue. You pause, knowing that you are hopelessly lost, without a clue as to which way you must go to find the Pharaoh's Beard and not very sure how to get back up to the main corridor and the door out.

You hold the ankh higher. "All right," you mutter. "Gods of Egypt, I need your help. I hope I haven't insulted you or anything. I don't know why you brought me here, but I'm willing to help you if you're willing to help me."

Your voice sounds muffled in the silent tomb, as though the stone walls themselves can swallow up the noise. A chill runs down your back, and you whirl around, but no one is there. The eyes of the statue appear to glitter in the ankh-light as you turn back to it.

The gods of Egypt, if there are any listening, aren't responding to your plea. You sigh.

A faint sound echoes as a sleek creature appears from behind the feet of the ebony statue, a dark-furred cat, as graceful as an otter. It approaches you and sits, large ears pricked, wrapping its tail about its feet. The slanted green eyes reflect the glow from the ankh.

"Matthew," the creature says, "I am from the goddess Bast, guardian of cats. Follow me, if you will."

While you catch your breath from the surprise of the talking animal, you look at it cautiously. You've never liked cats much . . . tricky and sly creatures. You prefer a dog, a great galumphing dog, always ready to hunt with you and slobber you with kisses when you're done. Cats are trouble.

On the other hand, you did ask the gods for help, and this is the only one that bothered to answer.

1. If you follow the cat, turn to Pathway 25 (page 119).

2. Seek out your answer in Pathway 8 (page 45) if you refuse the cat's help.

PATHWAY
21

Y ou push the sword into your belt and hold up your hands. "All right! What do you want with us?"

The tide of beetles pushes closer and closer to you, and you feel the sweat running down your brow. Could you have been wrong? Are you just about to be made beetle lunch?

Then the lead beetle halts, its antennae flexing. You stare at the ugly bug. You take a step foward, and it doesn't budge. You take a step backward, and it steps forward. Slowly, but surely, it backs you toward the steep ramp on the opposite side of the well.

Two or three of the gigantic creatures rear up, scrabbling at Ramses. You beckon him. "Come on down! They want both of us."

"Not on your life," the shepherd boy protests. He lets out a thin shriek as a beetle appears from behind him, lowers its head, and butts him over the side. He lands with a sickening crunch on top of a pile of dead beetles and gets up quickly, wading to your side.

"I'm with you," he says, with a shudder.

"This way then." You lead him up the ramp, the beetles waddling behind you, their shadows eerie monsters in the ankh-light as they herd you through the mystic pyramid.

The two of you are marched past dusty mysteries, coffins standing on end, statues guarding dead ends and false doors, and skeletons face down in the dirt. Ramses shudders again, muttering, "Robbers," while you merely wonder what it was that did them in—and will you have to face the same thing in the corridors ahead?

You face a pair of doors, long unsealed, and Ramses gasps, "Set!" as the beetles finally leave you, fading away in the many corridors.

You have no doubt they would quickly return if you tried to leave. You pull the carved doors open, ignoring the seals of evil, as Ramses gasps.

Inside is a great chamber, painted and decorated so it is fit for the Pharaoh himself. The rounded ceiling is painted dark blue with stars upon it, and a faint pathway traces the way of the crescent moon. The walls are decorated with pictures of the gods, and you are amazed at the fighting and slaying between them.

But you are not amazed to see the lovely Isis

seated, her hands bound in a rope that appears to be of curled darkness, and her face streaked with tears.

She looks up as the two of you step into the chamber. "Run," she begs you. "Run while you can. Set is here!"

"We can't leave you behind," you declare, pulling out your stained weapon once more.

"We can if she asks us to," mutters Ramses. "After all, she's immortal."

"But you sent the beetles for us."

She shakes her head, ripples of blue-black shining in the half-light thrown by your ankh and the clay lamps lining the walls. "No . . . they are the minions of Set. He is searching for you!"

At her side, you reach for the inky ropes bespelling her wrists.

She pulls her arms away. "You must do as I say. You must run, for when Osiris hears of this, and Horus and Neb and all the others, the heavens will rage. Always we are warring. Always!" A tear traces its way down her fine-boned cheek and falls to her lap, where it rolls into a pearl and drops to the dusty floor of the chamber.

Her eyes do not look upon it, but you realize she must need the ankh to get free. Your lips feel very dry suddenly as you lick them. To give

108

her the ankh is to give up your own hope of going home.

You look about you. The walls indeed depict an eternal struggle between the gods . . . ones in which no one seems to win and yet no one seems to lose. What can you do in such a situation? Isis has begged you to go.

1. *Will you give the ankh to Isis for her aid? If so, go to Pathway 5 (page 31).*

2. *Or will you use the ankh on yourself, to see if it will send you back, with Isis's presence to strengthen it? If this is your choice, turn to Pathway 35 (page 157).*

PATHWAY
22

"I didn't do anything," you cry, and you draw the sword, slashing at the knees of the vast being.

Suddenly the invisible force which held you gives way and the being disappears in a puff of smoke. Stumbling foward, you catch yourself on the sword like a cane.

Sir Hewbert was right! In triumph, you run into the night as far and fast as you can from the Valley of Kings and its tombs. By morning, you're footsore and hungry and thirsty, for even the night air is dry and parching. Your lips feel like scales. As the dawn lightens the sky to gray and then to blue, you look about you.

Before you can wonder if you will find water to survive, a roar splits the rocky wilderness. Its loudness shatters the blade of your sword as you

110

clasp your hands to your ears, deafened by the horrible noise.

A shadow falls over you, and you look up, unable to hear the sound the creature makes. A tremendous winged lion with the deformed face of a man descends upon you, its muzzle open and fangs glistening.

Helpless, your weapon destroyed, you crouch and wait for the sphinx to devour you.

IS THIS THE END?

PATHWAY
23

Y ou take a running leap and hit the wall, clawing frantically to gain toeholds and handholds. The giant beetles chitter and leap after you, their hairy legs scratching in vain on the clay walls, as you pull yourself up and onto the ledge.

Ramses dodges as you hack at the beetles behind him, hard shells smashing with every blow, until the gigantic scarabs collapse in a pool of gore on the ledge. You grab your friend and drag him past the battlefield and back into the maze of corridors.

"What now?"

You replace the sword in your hand with the ankh. Its aura still chases away the gloom, but it looks fainter to you.

"I'd say we're in trouble if this thing burns out! Look, it wanted me to go in to that sealed chamber down there. There must be another way in!"

Ramses purses his lips in thought, then gives a brisk nod. "We might be able to get in from above . . . . most of these chambers have secret exits, so that priests can go in, perform their rituals, and escape later." He points off in the dark at a narrow, crooked pathway. "That direction should do it."

You hold the ankh out. The tug is faint, for it really wishes you to go along the most direct route, but you try it anyway.

The passageway is tight. You and Ramses must turn sideways to squeeze through in several places, and with your tunic and mail coat on, you're even squarer than usual. Only the ankh keeps you going, for its tug becomes more and more insistent. Finally, you come to a halt as it determinedly points to a block of stone at the foot of the passageway.

Ramses gets on his stomach to look at it. A broken and grubby fingernail traces the block as he says, "Look here . . . this is a very wide crack, and it's not been mortared or anything. My guess is that it slides in or out."

You hand him down the sword, saying, "Be careful with the blade. That's our only weapon right now."

The shepherd boy nods and slides it gently between the stone surfaces, wiggling it steadily

113

until he has the top crevice cleaned. Then he does the same to the different sides, all but the bottom.

You take back the sword as he pauses, holding his breath.

"What are you waiting for?"

He looks up at you, black eyes solemn. "Did it ever occur to you that if I move this block, the whole wall could come down on us? We'd be crushed."

You look at the massive stonework. Throughout many of the passageways, the walls were plastered over for paintings. Carved columns appeared to hold up the walls at strategic places. Sometimes you had forgotten the deathtraps this building could hold for you. Then you take a deep breath. "There is a saying where I come from: He who hesitates is lost. Let's do it!"

With a grunt and a heave, Ramses pushes the stone as hard as he can. It budges the width of your hand and stops. You drop to your knees and push as well, the stone sliding farther and farther into the wall, until suddenly it is gone, crashing somewhere below.

The whole wall begins to shift as you catch your breath and scramble back to your feet, hauling Ramses up with you. If you're going down, you want to do it standing like a man!

The floor gently slopes, opening up into a ramp that takes you underneath the wall.

The two of you brace yourself and walk down carefully—into a chamber full of more treasures than you could ever possibly dream.

Ramses sinks to his knees in wonder, and then begins to cry silently, tears streaming down his bronzed face. "My mother, my father—my blind uncle! I could bring home enough for them to all live like kings! By all the gods . . ." And his voice trails off as he sits stunned, looking at the wonder.

And you know what he feels. The splendor here could outfit a hundred crusades to save the Holy Land. In all the world, you never dreamed there could be so much gold or precious jewels. Scented woods and delicate perfumed jars sit among urns of coins and gems. You stagger forward, looking at swords that, although made of bronze, show exquisite edges and designs in their guards and hilts. Your mouth is dry as you step through the treasure room. Ivory, ebony, rubies, emeralds, and more. What one man could have used all this wealth? And to think it was buried with him!

In the corner is a single black spear, made of jet. It draws you, and you remember that Isis is seeking the spear of Set. This must be it!

But as you approach it, you stumble over a bust, and the death mask of an Egyptian slips from it, and you see a strap holding on a false beard—but what a beard! Gold, no less, and lapis lazuli, and silver!

"The Pharaoh's Beard," Ramses gasps, pointing at the object you hold in your hand.

The ankh fairly buzzes with renewed power as the two draw very close together. You look at Ramses in triumph. "That's why the Sphinx wants this. It can repower an ankh!"

"Then the gods will have to give the Sphinx power, and take it into confidence in their schemes. It will have a measure of its own power."

"And Set, without his spear, will be easy for Isis to exile."

Ramses shakes his head. "It is hard to understand these wars. Our land is so dry and hard to live in . . . there must be other things better than power."

You agree with him, and ask yourself if these, or any of the other treasures, are worth taking.

1. Will you take the treasure out? If so, turn to Pathway 12 (page 63).

2. Will you leave the treasures behind? Go to Pathway 44 (page 183).

PATHWAY
24

As Set roars in a terrible temper, "Come here," you spring the other way, toward the urns and the dwarf god Bes. The dwarf pushes over a huge urn, and you hurdle it as he beckons you on.

"This way, this way!"

A shaft leads from behind the urn, and you plunge into it, running so quickly that the ankh's light is unpredictable, sometimes illuminating and sometimes blinding.

You run for your life, as something trails you. You can hear it shuffling and moaning, dragging itself through the passage after you. The dwarf god hops up and down as he waits for you to join him at a fork in the corridors. He points in glee, holding on to his headdress with the other hand.

"This way, this way, quickly! The mummy is after you!"

With a gasp for breath, you turn down the corridor, racing as fast as you can run. But the ankh throws out its golden light into a dead end, and you whirl around.

"Wait! This doesn't go anywhere!"

Your words of protest stop, as the gray-ragged monster looms in the corridor, with no way out behind it. The creature moans and groans in triumph, its hand groping for you.

Bes hops up and down in glee behind it, clapping his hands, as the mummy draws ever closer.

"But I—I thought you wanted to help me. You said you were the god of luck!" Your lips are dry as the eyeless, featureless, undead being touches your hand and draws you close, its evil slowly suffocating the light of the bronze ankh.

"I am, I am! But as any gambler knows, sometimes luck is good, and sometimes it's bad!"

THE END

PATHWAY
25

"I asked for help, and I guess I'd better take it," you reluctantly tell the feline. "I only hope you're more helpful than other cats I know have been."

Instead of taking offense, the seal-brown creature merely blinks its green eyes. "We cats have our own way of doing things," it says haughtily, and starts down a passageway with a flip of its tail.

"Yeah, like playing with mice before you eat them," you mutter under your breath before you start after it.

It picks a dusty passageway and minces through it as though upset to get its paws dirty. With a shrug, you follow closely, as it leads you deeper into the maze of the pyramid.

You trip over a loose stone, and the cat spits,

"Careful, fool! You'll bring the roof down on us!"

Righting yourself, you look upward in awe, at blocks that could easily crush a horse. You remembering Ramses's warning of the many death-traps in the pyramid, designed to discourage robbers.

"You wouldn't happen to know where the Pharaoh's Beard is?" you ask quietly.

"And what if I did?" answers the cat. "The Pharaoh wears it, not you."

"I was sent by a god to get it."

The cat stops, circles, and peers up at you. "Which god? Osiris? Isis? Horus?" Then it sniffs. "No matter. They never tell Bast anything. Very well, I will take you to the Beard, for the greater gods have instructed me to answer your request for help." Sleek tail waving like a flag, the cat turns around again and takes another passage-way, this one climbing up.

Puffing, you double-step to keep up with the agile feline, thinking that it doesn't know the Sphinx sent you after the Beard, and it's just as well. The gods of Egypt certainly seem to be fickle . . . and more than a little vain, if this Bast is anything to judge by. You just wish you were back, hoping to gain your knighthood in the crusades!

Up, up, and across, and then the cat stops,

stands on its hind legs, and scratches upon a sealed door. "If you fear not the curse," it says in a smug voice, "the Beard lies within."

Curse? A shiver runs down your spine, but you haven't any choice. With the edge of your sword, you chip off the seal, then pry the door open. The stone budges only when you throw all of your body weight behind it.

The ankh-light shines brilliantly within, and you gasp as you see the splendor of the Pharaoh's tomb. Chairs of embroidered cloth, chariots, boats, game boards, urns spilling over with gold and precious gems, many filled with dried grains and fruits—the chamber is a testimony to the richness of the life of the Pharaoh. No favorite object was left behind, even to stuffed cheetahs, a sleek hunting dog, and a cat much like the one waiting for you outside in the corridor.

You think of the war-horse and armor even a handful of this treasure would buy you, and your mouth dries. But this belongs to another man, even if he is dead now, and unless it is freely given, you don't want to take it. It's bad enough to take his Beard, whatever that might be.

"Inside!" the cat hisses and urges you to another sealed door. As you open it, the heavy scent of dead air perfumed with incenses and oils greets you. Even the ankh-light is subdued as you step into the burial chamber.

A huge coffin, laden with gold and lapis lazuli, sparkles in the twilight. Busts and other objects abound, and the room is painted with scenes of a beast-headed god welcoming the Pharaoh and guiding him to a boat, which then proceeds into a starry sky. You look at the huge coffin, nearly as high as yourself.

Other coffins and statues standing on end circle the room, but you ignore them. The treasures here are beyond compare, but you touch them not . . . for the coffin in the room's center holds the Pharaoh, and the death mask of the man bears the imprint of a beard.

The cat follows you in on whispering feet. "Lift the lid."

You shudder, thinking of the awful decay sure to face you. "No!"

"You must if you want the Beard."

Sword point again chips away a seal, and with a grunt and a heavy push, you lift the lid up. A second coffin lid greets you, and the death mask this time is not of gold and jewels, but a fine terra-cotta, painted, even to the eyes closed in eternal sleep, and you shudder, for it must be a very good portrait of the man within.

You pry open this lid. A bundle wrapped in cloth greets you, arms folded across the chest.

122

There is no evil smell or putrefaction, you realize with a grateful sigh, nor do you have to remove the final death mask, for this one has a false beard pulled onto it, a beard no less precious, for it is worked of gold and silver. You snatch it off and let the lid slam shut.

The main sarcophagus lid slides back into place after much protest. The Beard of the Pharaoh dangles from your hand as you raise the ankh for light, and a creak draws your attention.

A standing coffin lid opens slowly, as your feet freeze and your legs turn numb, unable to obey you. The wrapped being within lurches to its feet and totters out after you.

"A mummy!" The cat arches its back and scampers out ahead of you, spitting and fur on end. "It's here to guard the Pharaoh! Run for it!"

You draw your sword, hang the Beard on its thong around your neck, and edge out after the cat, chills running up and down your spine at the sight of the dead man wrapped in cloth pursuing you with low, eerie moans.

As you back down the corridor, it bats away your sword, impervious to the sharpness of the blade. All that happens is that a musty piece of cloth drifts to the corridor floor.

"What'll stop it?"

"Nothing!" yowls the cat. "This way! Jump for

it!" And it springs to a lever, hanging in midair by its claws, pulling the lever down.

With a grinding and a roar, the whole side of the pyramid opens, and you're on a ramp, sliding wildly downward, from nearly the top of the gigantic building.

You fall to the seat of your pants, and the cat slides past you, still nimble-footed, fur on end, as the ramp dumps you unceremoniously to the sands at the foot of the pyramid.

Without waiting to see if you're pursued, you jump up and race to the far side of the pyramid, looking for the wilderness beyond, and the great Sphinx.

"I have it! I have it!" you call, and pull the Beard from around your neck.

A roar sounds, and the Sphinx appears, wings spread, face in triumphant glee. "Then give it to me, mortal, and I will give you my secret of the ages!"

As you hand the Beard to the Sphinx, who puts it on and cries with triumph a second time, the heavy desert air rolls with thunder and splits with lightning. You whirl to see a cloud of gods bearing down upon you, their faces angry and their weapons raised. Set points, and a trio of mummies converge on you.

How can you hope to face the anger of the gods? The great Sphinx has evidently done something to incur their wrath, and only you stand between them. Will you fight to save the Sphinx, or run to save your own skin?

1. If you run, turn to Pathway 42 (page 179).
2. Look to Pathway 34 (page 155) if you fight to save the Sphinx.

PATHWAY
26

W ithout hesitation, together you cry, "The ramp!" and turn and dive headfirst onto the earthen ramp leading through the stone side of the pyramid.

For a moment, the blazing light of the outside stuns you, as the two of you slide downward, quicker and quicker. But Ramses shouts in triumph, for he has found one of the secret exits from the pyramid, and Set cannot follow you into the daylight.

You brace your boots to slow your slide as you look down to see the water and reeds below, and the ripple of dull-green scales. You tighten your grip on the sword.

"We're not out of this yet!" you shout, as jaws snap and prepare to receive you, like an offering from the gods.

"Crocodiles," screams Ramses in dismay, as the two of you tumble through the air, toward their gleaming white jaws.

CAN THIS BE THE END?

PATHWAY 27

You shake the ankh, crying, "Strike them dead! Give me your powers!" as the scarab beetles rear all around you, crying and chittering and rattling their armored backs.

With a flash, the ankh glows in your hand, hotter and hotter. A low whine grows, louder and stronger and higher in pitch until you scarcely think you can bear it. Suddenly, you throw the ankh down, unable to stand the heat or the sound any longer—and all the beetles about you collapse, and the great towering shadow behind you thuds like a fallen timber as you step aside.

The ankh continues to glow on the ground, and as you lean over to pick it up, Ramses cries out, "No, Matthew!"

Too late, for the weakened floor gives out under you and you plunge, down, down, down into darkness.

You pull the ankh from under you, and its feeble light shows that you are at the bottom of a chamber. Bundles of reeds are set into niches, and you quickly reach for one, to strike a fire with your flint and iron, for the power of the ankh is no longer enough to light your way . . . and may never be again. As you move, a panel snaps shut overhead.

In panic, you lift the ankh and see by its tiny glow that the ceiling has closed over you! Now even Ramses cannot help you.

You have fallen for many, many feet, but you landed in a huge straw basket of scrolls, which undoubtedly helped break your fall instead of a leg. As you roll out, you consider lighting a scroll for a torch, then change your mind. It would probably burn too quickly. You grab the tightly bound length of reeds, painstakingly strike a spark into its end, and nurse the bundle into flame.

It works well as a torch, though it's dry as tinder and burns too quickly. You take stock of the chamber and the other bundles, for you will need another torch soon, unless you can get out of here.

Five doors face you, or rather, four doors and a set of carved pillars with a curtain hanging between them. To your far left is a door with a jackal-headed god on it, and the ankh in your free hand helps you read the insignia in clay that has been scribed upon it.

"Enter the Gates of the Guardian Anubis, Guardian to the Doors of Death and Beyond and Final Judge."

You shudder. That sounds awful! As the torch sputters black smoke and orange flame, you look at the next door. It is double-width, of smooth ebony wood, a door that any king would pay a fortune to have in his castle. Not a pictograph or word graces it.

The middle door is the pillars, carved to look like blossoms upon a stem, ever blooming and reaching upward. The curtain hanging between them is woven from reeds, painted depicting a river with a huge brown beast sunning itself, and a long-legged bird walking along the bank. You look at the piglike beast and wonder what it can be.

The next door is one of bronze, struck with the symbol of a war chariot, its yoke empty.

And the last door, the one on your far right, you have only a bare glimpse of before the torch gutters out, but you see it is carved from precious ivory, and shows the bust of a long-necked and beautiful woman, her hair bound high under her crownlike hat.

Quickly you light another bundle of reeds. As you do, you scuff up the basket of scrolls, which rolls aside to reveal tiles set down in the floor, inscribed with a message, and you read:

"Choose wisely. There is only one way out."

A piercing scream splits the air, and a horrible growling follows it, as the wooden ceiling above you bulges and threatens to come down again, dumping heaven knows what monsters on your head!

In panic, you take a deep breath and plunge headfirst across the room through an opening.

1. *If you go through the ebony door, turn to Pathway 31 (page 145).*

2. *If you choose Pathway 36 (page 160), you have chosen the pillars.*

3. *Go to Pathway 16 (page 82) if you open the bronze doors.*

4. *Find your destiny in Pathway 41 (page 175) if you choose the doors of death.*

5. *If the ivory doors are your decision, journey to Pathway 4 (page 28).*

PATHWAY
28

T he roaring of Set is almost enough to drown
your words as you raise the scroll and repeat
haltingly the incantation to awaken Anubis. As the
last word fades, the scroll is nothing but rough,
blank paper, and you drop it in amazement.

The god of death rises slowly, ponderously to
his feet, and you yelp and jump across the room,
just as Set crashes in, grasping to catch hold of
you.

The two beings face each other, eyes glittering in the twilight, and you think how similar
and dissimilar they look, for both wear doglike
headdresses, of a savage hunter and scavenger,
but there the similarity ends, for Set is mighty-
thewed, and Anubis is slender. He radiates a
kind of serenity and finality about him, and you
shudder, for you recognize the aura of death
and eternity.

"Pass no farther, Set. This is my domain. I am the guardian here."

"Give me the boy! He ridiculed me in front of Isis and Ra, and deserves my anger!"

Anubis laughs ironically. "You ridicule yourself, with your constant plots and warring. You can never win, as can they. Remember the balance, Set, above all!"

The god of evil clenches and unclenches his huge fists, then turns away. When he is gone, the god of death turns to you.

"And you are not part of the balance, boy. What are you doing here, within the eternal sphere of the pyramid?"

"I . . . I found an ankh, and it drew me here . . . even through time, a blind man told me, and the Sphinx agreed, and said if I got it the Pharaoh's Beard, it would send me back."

Anubis laughs as the words tumble out of your mouth, and you haven't even time to be amazed that, without the ankh, you are still being understood. "My brothers and sisters play their games of life and war, while I stay in final judgment. You have been drawn in by Isis's attempt to regain her ankh of power, one of the seven great ankhs. Now your part is done. I will send you back. Lie down in the boat here."

Your heart thuds in your chest. The boat he wishes you to occupy is a death boat . . . you recognize it from the hieroglyphs on the funeral chamber wall. Only the dead are supposed to occupy it.

"Uh . . ."

Anubis inclines his head and beckons with his staff. " Be quick about it, boy, lest Set return with his minions to pick a fight with me."

You clamber into the wooden boat and lie down, feeling stiff and cold. The jackal-headed god leans over you and motions with his staff. A wind rushes through the chamber, putting out the lamps, and you are left in darkness. You shiver, closing your eyes in fear.

The rocking of the boat makes you open your eyes, and you clutch the side. But stars meet your glance, and the spray of the ocean, and the eerie glow of waves at night under a moon. You sit up. You're in a dinghy!

You stand up with a shout of joy, as you see the outline of a large ship within hailing distance and begin to shout with all your might— for you recognize that ship and the flag it flies, even under the eerie light of a crescent moon. You're home!

THIS IS THE END OF YOUR ADVENTURE.

PATHWAY
29

Run now, think later, your feet tell you, as you find yourself running as fast as you can, scrambling over the rock and sand, leaving behind the screams and moans of the tomb robbers, as a tremendous blast shatters the air.

It knocks you to your knees. As you pitch yourself over the ridge top, tearing for a handhold in the sand, you run into an invisible wall, a force you cannot pierce, and you stagger to a halt, blinking in confusion. There's nothing to stop you—but you can't go on. You yank off the shepherd's robe you've worn for days to conceal your crusader's tunic and trousers and throw it on the ground.

A tremendous being materializes in front of you, feet spread in mighty stance. He bends low to look at you, amusement in his doglike eyes, a jackal headdress on the shoulders and body of a powerful man. Your heart thumps in your chest. What kind of demon is this?

"I am Anubis," the being says in answer to your unspoken question. "Guardian of the paths of the dead. Some also call me judge. You broke the sacred seals of the tomb of the Pharaoh."

You are caught by the gods themselves! You find your voice and manage to blurt out, "That wasn't me! That was Ahmed. In fact, most of us didn't even know what he was planning to do."

A misty whiteness grows in the air past his shoulders. It carries with it a delicate perfume, and your heart skips a beat, then slows in wonder. Out of the scented cloud, a woman speaks. Gods, it appears, come in all sizes. "What he says is true, Anubis."

The jackal head turns to look behind briefly, and you have the faint vision of a lovely woman reclining on a cloud of perfume as if it were a couch, fanning herself languidly. She has long black hair and wide almond-shaped eyes, and she smiles as she realizes you've seen her.

"Fair Isis," the jackal being says. "Do you wish mercy?"

The lady laughs gently. "I will not cross you, Anubis, not for all the dates in Egypt, for you are the judge of us all! No, do as you wish. Only I say that as evil intentions go, this boy is remarkably free of them."

The jackal-headed being shrugs, as the perfume cloud disappears, and the two of you are alone on the ridge overlooking the Valley of Kings. Moans issue from behind you, and cries for help, a scream cut short, and you wonder what has happened to Ahmed and his gang of tomb robbers, then decide you don't really want to know. You straighten your tunic.

A weight on your belt reminds you that you still bear your master's short if somewhat dull sword. You also remember Sir Hewbert's telling you that many a demon has fled at the sight and touch of cold steel.

Anubis says to you, in his great and yet solemn voice, "You are part of the whole that broke into the tomb, committing sacrilege, and for this you must pay. If you wish to fight the curse, you may, by undertaking a quest I will give you, a quest to aid a boy much like yourself, in centuries past—or you may take the punishment of the curse."

"And if I take the quest and win?" Your cold fingers curl about the hilt of the sword and find the bindings, worn by Hewbert's hand, comforting.

"You will be returned to wherever you came from," the god of death promises you.

A chance to go home, after all! But your thoughts roll around in your mind. You're innocent . . . why should this demon from another land judge your actions? With a weapon in your hands, you're as good as he is.

1. If you decide to fight the curse and take on the quest, go to Pathway 9 (page 49).
2. But if you pull your sword and attack the Egyptian god, turn to Pathway 22 (page 110).

PATHWAY
30

"**S**phinx, hear me!" you cry out, clutching at the ankh desperately with one hand and your sword with the other, as Apep rises and begins to sway, fangs glistening with green poison. "Come answer me as you promised!"

You dodge as Apep strikes. Stone powders at the force of the fangs hitting it. The snake pulls back hissing and writhing, and you shudder as its multicolored scales flex with the recoiling of its body. The slanted eyes look at you with hatred.

Ka-boom! The air shatters and you stagger back, ears protesting with a loud ringing, as a tawny body suddenly hangs in the air over you, wings beating and tufted tail lashing. The great Sphinx shadows you, a ferocious grimace on its feline face, claws extending as though to rip the very air apart.

140

Then it looks down and sees you, crying, "There you are, my little master! No riddling this time, for I owe you."

"Drive away Apep," you shout at the beast, and the Sphinx lets out a roar that nearly deafens you, and sweat runs down your face as you fight off the pain of the sound. Isis shivers behind you.

"You asked for another favor when first we met. Do you not wish to return to your own domain?"

"I'll worry about that later! For myself and the Lady Isis, drive the serpent away!"

The Sphinx smiles enigmatically. "For the goddess, anything." It bats its wings, extends them, and with a shriek, dives at the hissing reptile.

A horrendous screeching fills the chamber as Apep whips its body loose from the ground and throws its coils over the form of the Sphinx. The two tumble forward and back, howling at one another. The tawny form of the Sphinx bites and tears with a ferocity that makes you gulp and stagger away, drawing the goddess with you, to the safety of the staircase. That could have been you, had you not answered the riddle!

The Sphinx pulls free and lunges upward, to the top of the tall chamber, then plunges down, all four paws rigid, claws glistening like ivory daggers. Apep sits and strikes, missing, as the Sphinx grabs it by the back of the head.

Wailing and shrieking in its fury, the Sphinx spreads its wings and beats desperately to rise in the air, drawing the serpent upward in its claws. It rips and shreds Apep's flesh, sending gobs of blood and meat flying. You raise your arm to protect your face, for the blood sizzles when it hits the dirt, and the flesh lies in smoking chunks.

The weight of the snake tears it away, and the Sphinx shoots up suddenly as Apep rips loose, dropping back to the ground, where it coils tightly and strikes at its eternal foe.

The Sphinx lets out a high thin wail, as the serpent grabs it by the throat and shakes it, then spits it out on the earth. The creature lies there feebly, batting its wings and thrashing as the evil grinning head of Apep slithers close, to deliver a death strike, poison streaming down its fangs.

As the snake closes, you grip your sword tightly, prepared to finish off what the Sphinx started, your heart pounding in your chest.

Catlike, the Sphinx bounds up and lands on the serpent's head, tearing at the great slanted eyes. Apep spits and shakes its head, and with a loud hissing, sinks quickly into the earth, drawing its coils after it, as the dirt settles over its body.

As quickly as it had erupted into the chamber, the great serpent is gone!

The Sphinx settles to the ground with a cry, staggers toward the two of you, and collapses limply upon its haunches.

You run to it, Isis at your heels, and you gently smooth the tangled mane of hair from its face.

"I am dying, man," the Sphinx moans. "But your riddle is answered."

Isis lays her slender hand over yours on the head of the Sphinx. "No creature dies in vain serving me. I am not yet mighty enough to drive the venom from you, Sphinx, but I will save your life and grant you immortality, for your stone figure will grace the sands for time immemorial, until I release and heal you."

With those words, the form of the Sphinx melts away from your hand and your sight and you are holding only the air.

"What do you mean? What did you do?"

Isis smiles. "The Sphinx, in stone form, will look over these sands as long as the rock withstands time. With the help of one of my brothers, I will one day heal it in gratitude. As for you, champion of my ankh, the Sphinx mentioned owing you another debt, and you disclaimed it to save me from Apep. What is it you had asked of the beast?"

"I, ah, well . . . I was brought here by the ankh from another land and another time. I'm a page to Sir Hewbert, and we were traveling to free Jerusalem and the Holy Lands. The Sphinx said she could send me back, if I brought her the Pharaoh's Beard."

Gentle laughter sounds from her curved lips. "Not so humble a beast as I thought! The Sphinx was buying power of its own, then. Well, perhaps it may be stone a little longer than I planned for such insolence, but I will fulfill its promise to you. When you awaken, you will be at your master's side, wherever that may be. Close your eyes tightly and think of Sir Hewbert."

Gripping the sword, you do as the goddess bids, and as the gut-wrenching darkness of travel by ankh takes you, you feel its weight slip from your belt forever.

THIS IS THE END OF THIS PATHWAY.

PATHWAY
31

Y ou land face first in total darkness, as a strange wind blows across your back, snuffing out all light or hope of light. The ankh's weak light flickers from your hand as you hold it up.

This is not the place you want to be! Ebony doors block your exit as you scramble up in panic, for the center of the room is a pit, a boiling pit of ebony bodies, coiling and hissing and tumbling to hiss at you.

Snakes!

You can't control the scream that is torn from you as something droops from the chamber ceiling, brushing across your face and then dropping into the pit, to coil and recoil with its reptile brothers. A sweat breaks out, and you find yourself shaking all over like a frightened child, afraid to move a step one way or another.

You put an arm out to steady yourself and jerk it back as the wall hisses! With a gulp, you pivot slightly and see that the whole room is alive, alive with slithering bodies!

The ankh sheds a beam of light across a carved plaque, and you read: "Welcome to the Pharaoh's Chamber of Horros."

You gulp and steady yourself by putting your hand on your sword hilt. If need be, you can cut your way out!

If one of the vipers doesn't strike you first.

A bead of sweat slowly runs down your forehead as you inch your way along the rim of the pit, headed for what looks like another door at the other side of the chamber.

You freeze as a reptile drops down upon your shoulder, slithers around your neck onto your other shoulder, follows the length of your out-stretched arm, and drops into the pit as nonchalantly as if it had been out for a stroll. You groan and bite back the vomit in your throat.

Inch by inch, hiss by threatening hiss, you work your way toward the freedom of the doors.

Ssssst! A huge snake rears up, flaplike wings at the side of its head, forked tongue writhing as it sways to and fro. You can't help it any longer. In sheer panic, you lop its head off and watch the body go flopping downward, where its mates eagerly devour its remains. You belt the sword and dive headfirst for the set of doors.

Turn to Pathway 4 (page 28).

PATHWAY
32

Y ou take Ramses by the shoulder. "If you can lead me in, I say let's look for your father now. The high priests probably left him here—it would be too risky to take him to where the Pharaoh is being prepared."

The boy swallows, and you can tell he's afraid, but he says bravely, "The gods will surely not mind—after all, they sent you to help me."

At that, he turns back to the sands, and you pick up the waterskin and follow him, wondering if you feel as brave as he does.

As you step about the edge of the pyramid, you can feel its towering vastness above you, and you look across the red-gold sands, far away. You can see buildings on the horizon.

"That is the city of the dead," Ramses says. "And across the river is my city."

Thinking that the Egyptians have strange cus-

149

toms, you shoulder the waterskin and look at the earthen ramp leading up to a dark entrance in the pyramid's base. Ramses walks ahead of you, his steps kicking up puffs of dirt, and you follow.

"It must have taken a lot of slaves to build this thing," you say, but the ankh has twisted your words a little, for you said "serfs."

Ramses shakes his head with a funny laugh. "Slaves! No, an army of free men built this. They have worked on it for over thirty years, each section built by a different group of men and artists. They were all anxious to partake in the glory of this gift to the gods, and have their talents known. This is the only creation of its kind."

You look around with a low whistle as you step into the carved corridor. "Well, I'll bet somebody else builds more. Look at this!" The desert sun, which was threatening to grow hot and sullen, is defeated by the thick stone walls of the building as the two of you walk through.

Ramses has taken a small clay lamp from its niche near the front and is holding it out to illuminate your passage, and similar lamps waver as the two of you pass.

The walls are covered with paintings, flat paintings that show only the sides of people, reminding you of stick drawings you used to do in the mud flats near your favorite swimming hole.

150

But these paintings are different in that they are colorful and decorative and show a story of a kind.

Ramses turns down a side corridor, and you follow. His voice is faint as he says, "Be careful."

You are too busy gawking at the sights to notice that he steps over a stone set into the floor. You trip on it, bumping forward into Ramses, yelling, "Look out!"

Too late. The wall moves with a grinding sound, dumping the two of you downward suddenly, tumbling you over each other again and again, plunging you into darkness.

The little orange lamp flame sputters back into life as the two of you come to a halt at the bottom of a shaft. Above you, just out of reach, is a lever sticking from the wall. Ramses scrambles to his feet, shouting in panic, and soon you understand why.

Sand. Sand is pouring out of holes in the walls, and before you can even shout, you are up to your knees in the fine grains. "Get up on my shoulder, Ramses, and pull the lever!"

"No, my friend—it may make things worse!"

The sand showers about you, now up to your waist, raising a dust that threatens to choke you as well. You wade next to him before you are so buried that you can't move.

As you ponderously swim your body through the heavy sand, the ankh swings around your neck. It had magical powers before, and you are on a quest—maybe it can save the two of you now.

You draw it out, your eyes stinging from the powdery sand, and hold it up. Ramses is standing very still, his arms frozen to his sides, hands and elbows hidden by the sand. He looks at you.

"What are you going to do?"

The ankh feels heavy in your hands. You can't reach the lever by yourself, but you can throw the ankh, and if you're lucky, its weight will pull the lever down.

Or you can simply try to invoke its powers to save the two of you. But there's no time to hesitate, for the sand is now up to Ramses's chin and your arms will be free only a short time longer!

1. *If you throw the ankh at the lever, turn to Pathway 17 (page 84).*

2. *Go to Pathway 2 (page 24) if you invoke the ankh's powers.*

PATHWAY
33

Y ou throw the scroll at the evil god Set as he bursts through the second pair of doors, and you draw your sword. The god slows down only long enough to laugh heartily at your gesture, and then he reaches for you with the mighty arms of a born warrior.

You slash across his left arm, the blade cutting deep and clean, and fall back in astonishment as the god yowls in pain and staggers back, sparks and smoke fountaining up from his wound! The crimson cross on your tunic seems to glow with life, and the white background sends out a light of its own.

You stand in amazement as the god falls to his knees crying in a tongue which grows incoherent to you, and the funeral chamber begins to swirl around you in a fog. A soft voice calls after you, "Thank you for the return of the ankh . . . more than this can never be!"

And you are awash on the deck of your ship, digging the sword point deep into the wood to save yourself, just as Sir Hewbert catches hold of your tunic and you are saved from going overboard. You blink, as a scroll of paper floats past you and is gone in a spray of seawater.

THE END

PATHWAY
34

W ithout hesitation, you hurl yourself at the mummies, for the Sphinx has promised you a way back. You pull Sir Hewbert's sword, crying in defiance, "For the Holy Lands!" You add, over your shoulder, "Do whatever it is you have to do to send me back!"

The Sphinx settles on its haunches and closes its eyes, its lips moving in recitation to whatever spell it is working on. You whirl around, just as a mummy bats at you, knocking you off your feet.

You roll away as it tries to stomp on you, its dusty bandages flapping. You bound up, and duck as the second one lunges at you, and it vaults over your back, knocking the first flat to the sands. The two of them tumble together blindly as you mutter, "Two down, one to go.

155

Hurry up!" The thunders rumble ever more threateningly as the cloud of gods draws closer.

The Sphinx's eyes open wide, and it smiles. "Farewell, little mortal . . . for you have given me the power to become one of the lesser gods myself!"

You rise into the air, shouting, "Hey!" and then you feel yourself growing fainter and fainter, as the mummies dance vainly below you.

The last sight you see is the cloud of gods ringing the Sphinx, as a bolt of their power strikes it, turning it instantly into stone. Sadness mingles with joy, as you smell the sharp tang of salt air and find yourself about to plunge into the water, just off the prow of the boat, as Sir Hewbert leans over yelling, "Man overboard! Don't worry, lad. I'll save you!"

THIS IS THE END OF YOUR ADVENTURE.

PATHWAY
35

Y ou swallow, and say, "Lady Isis . . . you are a lady in distress if I ever met one—but everything inside this pyramid has shown me that you gods make most of the trouble for yourselves! This ankh brought me here, and the Sphinx has promised to send me back if I bring her the Pharaoh's Beard and help you . . . but I think you could send me back, too, if you wanted."

Her wide eyes regard you. Then she nods. "Indeed I could. If I wished."

The air inside the chamber trembles. Ramses whispers, "Hurry, Matthew! I think Set is returning!"

"Then send me back—but keep your hand on the ankh, so that you can pull it back with you! Then we will both have what we want."

Isis looks very solemn, a fine line between her brows as she considers your words.

A growling and a thud of heavy footsteps stop you, and you and Ramses turn as the chamber doors are thrown up. Great Set, god of evil and darkness, glowers in the doorway, a vicious hyena mask his headdress! Twisted black figures caper behind him, vicious beasts and grayed mummies.

"Isis! I have you and now your power!"

The goddess thrusts herself to her feet proudly, lifting her chin in defiance. "By Ra and Osiris, you have no one!" she calls.

The air thunders, as two more countenances look down. "You summon us, fair sister?"

Ramses gasps. "Ra, the sun-god! And Osiris, the avenger!"

If you're going to escape this battle, it's now or never! You hold the ankh in front of Isis.

"Goddess! Send us back! The wars of gods were never meant for mortals to see," you plead.

Her hands close over yours as she chants, and you can feel the room swirling away, your guts twisting in a dark you cannot see through, and your ears pierced with a ringing.

With a whoosh, your eyes and ears clear, and you thump down to a baked plain. Horses rear, and crusaders curb them in place, armor creaks and rattles, and a hearty voice calls out, "Matthew! What black magic is this?"

You turn and see that the gods of Egypt have followed you, shouting and yelling at each other!

You hold your head with a groan. What a mess this is going to be to straighten out—and how will you explain it to Sir Hewbert?

THIS IS THE END OF YOUR ADVENTURE.

PATHWAY
36

T he reed curtain drops into place behind you as you plunge into twilight, only the ankh in your hand giving out light. Wind whistles through your hair as you stand uncertainly. It is wet in here, and water is pooled about the floor, hiding your boots almost all the way to their tops.

Unsure if you are any better off, you take a hesitant step. Instantly, the floor flexes under your feet, as a gigantic pair of jaws takes a snap and you jump with a yelp!

The ankh-light gleams, as a green-scaled beast thrashes, whipping its tail around. You hop for the other side of the pond, where there are another set of pillars and a reed curtain hanging across an exit.

The scaled beasts are all over, sliding eagerly toward your flashing legs. Their long jaws snap and clack as they hiss like angry cats. Dragons

they are, long-bodied, green-scaled dragons, with immense jaws.

They are coming for you, too, bellowing with a hunger that must be more immortal than they themselves. Ignoring caution, you run for the other side, right across the backs of the squat dragonish beasts, even as they bellow and hiss and whip their tails to catch you!

With a sigh of relief, you lean upon the reed curtain and pillar for balance . . . then see the dragons coming after you!

As you jump back in surprise, the pillar collapses, throwing you into pure and utter darkness.

Go to Pathway 16 (page 82).

PATHWAY
37

Y̲ou bow to Isis and hand her the spear, the ankh, and the Beard. Isis's face flushes with pleasure, and she bows her head deeply.

"You can't know the depth of my feelings, champion of the ankh," she says. "The Sphinx is a wily beast, but one of chaos. It would be truly dangerous and almost godlike with the Beard. It never had the power to send you home, but it did have the power to send you on a perilous quest."

The Sphinx drops its head with a low growl and examines its unvelveted claws.

Isis looks at it. "It knows the Beard and the ankh would have summoned me. But look at this!" And she puts the two objects together, and they glow, and as she draws them apart, the sun beams down, washing them in its rays, connecting all of them in a triangle of solar power. As suddenly, the triangle winks out.

"The great ankh is now fully powered again, and I can take my rightful place in the balance of things. The Sphinx's power is that it knows how to make others feel that it has power."

You bite your lip, happy that you have correctly guessed the creature's secret. Ramses stands with his mouth slightly open, drinking in the words of his goddess.

"And as for you . . . I grant that the Sphinx will indeed take you home. It will be a long and turbulent flight, Sphinx, but bear him well—or you will hear from me."

Isis commands you to mount the beast and bury your hands in its mane for steadiness. The creature beats its wings greatly, and you rise above the sands.

"What about Ramses?" you call down.

Isis smiles. "I will see him home, and in gratitude for his part, I can guarantee you that there will be a pharaoh or two in the future named Ramses."

With that, she waves her hand, and the Sphinx springs into the air with a roar and a growl. Soon you are winging your way over the exotic sands of ancient Egypt, wondering what your fellow crusaders will do when you and a Sphinx suddenly show up.

THE END

PATHWAY
38

As Apep rears back for a strike, you grab Isis's hand. "Goddess or not, I'm not big enough to fight that thing!" Leaping the steps two at a time, you run for your life up the staircase, shielding the woman with your own body as the serpent furiously strikes at you, hitting the stone steps just short each time.

At the top, you push her through the archway, slash one time at the serpent's eyes as it threatens to follow, and bolt after her.

Like a tea kettle torn loose, the corridor fills with boiling and hissing and spitting as Isis pauses, narrows her brows, and points at a blank spot on the corridor wall. A stone swings open. You're happy to follow her, for the pit of snakes is answering Apep's fury, and you're not at all eager to swing over them again.

As Isis flees down the cool corridor, you're aware of the incense burning in the lamps along the dim tunnel. Her white gown drags the ground as her slender feet hurry, covered by the barest of golden sandals. Her raven-dark hair swings along the gentle curve of her back, and you think that you'll never, ever see anyone as beautiful as she.

At the corridor's end, two gigantic statues guard a double door, their arms folded across their chests, one holding a plumed fan and the other an ankh similar to your own. At her soft voice, the plumed fan and ankh move aside and the door opens.

A golden glow bathes the two of you, and all the fear and hurt of the day's battle floods away. You feel ten feet tall and heroic as well, as you return the sword to its place in your belt.

Isis turns. She takes the ankh from you gently, saying, "Thank you, my hero, for bearing this back to me. I have need of a champion, and you, though your blue eyes are strange to me, are well-featured and brave. Stay with me and be my Champion. I cannot give you immortality, but I can promise you many more years than you would normally live, and many great adventures, for the gods of Egypt are always striving."

Your heart soars. Never would you serve a more beautiful mistress, nor hope for greater glory than this! "I'll stay with you forever," you pledge, as you drop to one knee at her side, and the golden glow encompasses both of you, removing you from the mystic pyramid and taking you to the ephemeral plane of the gods.

THE END

PATHWAY
39

Y ou check your belt to make sure the short sword is still there. "I say we find those priests and make them tell us where your father is!"

"Alone, I wouldn't dare," Ramses agrees, his eyes flashing. "But now you're here to help!"

You don't feel quite that brave, in the shadow of the great pyramid, but you're determined to do the best you can. Anything to get rid of the curse and get home again!

It is late afternoon and you've finished off the waterskin when Ramses hears a noise. He jumps up. "Listen!" He steps to the edge and looks about carefully.

"It's them! A whole procession, coming to the pyramid."

You join him and see the men walking across the sand, dressed in the pleated skirts and sandals you are used to seeing now. Necklaces of gold and stones adorn their bare chests. Slaves follow, waving immense fans on sticks, to keep the sun from their shaved heads. Their noses are hawklike, and you sense an immediate dislike. These men are powerful, and you can feel Ramses's fear.

"We'll let them go in . . . all but the last two," you decide.

"And then what?"

"We pull them off the ramp and force them to tell us where your father is!" You feel somewhat bolder, having seen that the priests have little in the way of weapons, except for ornamental ones. You watch as the slaves are dismissed and the priests talk quietly among themselves. You think that Ramses's father may be secreted somewhere inside. You watch as the priests walk slowly up the ramp.

True to your word, you dart from around the corner and grab at the ankles of the last priest going up the ramp, a stocky man with rolls of flesh hanging over the waist of his ceremonial dress. He falls with an *ooof!* but not before calling, "Help!" to the others.

"Now you've done it," Ramses declares. He jumps to the entrance ramp as the dark mouth of the pyramid boils with activity.

You pull the short sword from your belt. "Stay

behind me," you order, remembering your training as a page.

But Ramses bolts ahead, crying, "I know my father's in there somewhere!"

The priests scatter in confusion as he bulls his way through them, and you follow after.

Now you're inside the dark shadowy pyramid, and the priests are between you and freedom. You grab Ramses's sleeve as he pulls a lamp from a niche in the wall. "Wait a minute—do you know where you're going?"

"No, but—"

His sentence is never finished as voices call from the outside, and you hear clearly, "Set! O great Set! Come avenge this desecration to your sacred order!"

Ramses's hand shakes, and the flame in the clay lamp quivers.

"Who is this Set?" you mutter.

He falls to his knees. "The most wicked god of all—and most powerful! God of darkness and death and destruction!"

You pull him to his feet. "Well, I don't believe in him, so get up and let's find a way out out of here."

An angry cloud of whirling black blocks off your view of the sands beyond, and Ramses does as you bid, turning and running for his life down the corridor, crying out in fear. You follow, Sir Hewbert's tunic flapping about your legs as you do.

The buzz of angry hornets and cruel laughter follows you. Ramses leads you through twists and turns and corridors full of painted figures showing life along the Nile, and victories of the Pharaoh's armies, and the gods themselves, until at last you stand panting by a ramp.

"What's that?"

"A way out—I think. It is on the far side of the pyramid, down by the rushes and reeds where the ditches were cut to let the Nile run here, and the big blocks were ferried on these waterways."

"You mean there's a river there?"

"Not the real river. Just an arm of it."

"What are we waiting for?"

Ramses stands, his eyes growing wide with fright as he looks over your shoulder and the cruel laughter booms about you. He stammers. "Because I—I'm not sure—"

You spin around, as the gigantic figure of a warrior blocks the corridor, dark monstrous beings dancing around him—no, *it*—for the god has the head of a demon you've never seen before, cruel and doglike.

"Set," murmurs Ramses faintly, and you think you're going to lose him.

You grip your sword as snakes and wicked beasts boil about the evil god's ankles. "We've only got two choices, Ramses. Fight—or take that ramp of yours!"

1. *If you take the ramp, go to Pathway 26 (page 127).*

2. *But if you stand and fight, turn to Pathway 13 (page 67).*

PATHWAY
40

Y ou hand the Beard and the ankh to the Sphinx, and after long thought, the spear to Isis. She throws it angrily on the ground.

"Give me the Beard and the ankh—and then I can destroy Set."

"I think not," the Sphinx says sadly. "I will keep your objects of power, for all you have done, all you gods, is war among yourselves."

Isis stamps her sandaled foot upon the ground, and a high flush rises on her cheekbones. "What do you know, you gross smelly *beast*?"

You step between the feuding pair. "I think the Sphinx knows a great deal about me. The riddle it asks to determine a man's worth is not about gods or war . . . but about a man's life. It may be a beast now, but I think it was once— and still is—a very wise being. So wise, perhaps, that one of your gods changed it into the

Sphinx to punish it. Its words are harsh, and I doubt you liked listening to it very much. And now, with the ankh and the beard, it can turn itself back."

The Sphinx looks at you, and a slow smile curves its lips. "You have wisdom beyond your years, young master. I will not tell you if you are right or wrong about my being wise . . . after all, I ended up in this predicament. However, you have a world of your own to return to." It draws the thong about its head, centering the Pharaoh's Beard upon its chin. Instantly, the bronze ankh glows, and its oval head forms a golden sphere, much like the one Isis materialized from. "First you, and then your friend, back to your families."

Excited, you step into the bubble, but not before Ramses grabs you and hugs you good-bye. "Like kings," he whispers in your ears. "There are not words enough to thank you!"

Your heart aglow for having helped make his life better, you put your chin up and prepare to be returned to a glorious life as a crusader.

THE END

PATHWAY
41

As you crash through the door, the seal pops, and air explodes with a lightninglike flash, and you lie dazed on the floor.

The door closes behind you. Its noise is one of totality, and you think of the closing of a stone tomb.

With a gulp, you sit up, for the eerie wind whistling through the place makes it impossible for any torch to stay lit. You pull out the ankh, happy for even its dim flicker.

Spookiness is not the only problem with this room, you think with a shiver, hugging the tunic to you. For the first time since your adventure began, you are cold, stone-cold, ice-cold.

As cold as death, you think, as you force yourself to stand up, for your very joints are aching.

This was not a good idea, you decide as you

swing around and see the doors closed firmly behind you. And as you turn back around, you can see there is definitely no way out.

You lick your dry lips. There are pillars around all the sides, and they hold up what appears to be a bowl of the heavens, painted and starred by the artists. But the most remarkable portrait of all is the statue in front of you, the statue of a man with the headdress of a jackal from the shoulders up. It is difficult to see if it really is a statue or just might be alive.

"Hah!" you laugh softly to yourself and finish turning around, to see if you can fathom another way in or out. You push on the heavy stone door again, but it doesn't budge. You sigh and look toward Anubis, god of death and the final judge. "If I ever get out of here," you say, and your words echo in the cold room, "I'll never make fun of Sir Hewbert's belly again. Or anything else about him."

For comfort, you pat the hilt of his sword, hold the ankh higher, and go near the statue to inspect it.

As the gleam from the ankh strikes the eye of the jackal, the being moves.

You scream, dropping the ankh.

Anubis stands stiffly and looks down at you from his pedestal of a throne. "Who summons me?"

"I—ah—not me!" you cry, as you get down on your knees and frantically gather up the ankh.

The being regards you as you straighten. Then it says scornfully, "You are not dead."

"No! That is, not yet, anyway. Maybe any minute now, if I can't get out of here, but no . . . not yet." You clear your throat in embarrassment.

"Only the dead can pass my portals," the god says, waving a hand at you. "Be gone to your own place."

"But wa—" you gasp, as smoke fills the room, and you shoot into the air with a *whoosh!*

Your breath leaves your lungs and tears stain your face, as you grasp both the ankh and the sword for dear life. You didn't even get a chance to tell him where you wanted to go!

Not that that matters, for suddenly you feel the cold wetness of sea spray, and the cry of a gull, and the creak of a ship bucking a sudden Mediterranean storm.

You're home!

THIS IS THE END OF YOUR ADVENTURE.

PATHWAY
42

Without a second thought, you run, but the cloud of gods descends on the two of you with a rumble and a *poof!*

You find yourself frozen to the sands, crouched on cat haunches, looking out over the pyramids, a lesser version of the great stone Sphinx at your side, Pharaoh's Beard and all.

There you will await the sands of time, forever.

THE END

PATHWAY
43

⟨decorative divider⟩

Y ou pull the ankh from your belt and hold it high, crying, "Help Isis, please!"

A roar issues through the chamber, and a blinding flash of light strikes, knocking the ankh from your hand. From the golden splendor a being appears, a magnificent being with the headdress of an eagle head, radiating with golden spears of light.

Isis jumps from her couch, crying with happiness, "Ra!"

Set hurdles the couch with a snarled oath and throws the jet-black spear that he carries. It smashes into a thousand splinters at Ra's feet, and the golden god laughs in triumph.

"Darkness can never overcome the sun!"

But you stagger back, for you are directly in the path of the fleeing Set, as the evil god takes the stairs two and three at a time, and the earth

180

moans at the touch of his evil. Desperately, you grab for balance, and as you do, you touch an insignia placed into the wall, and a passageway opens up.

It is lit with clay lamps, and you scurry down the corridor. Set roars in fury, and you know that he has seen you!

Stairs lead you downward and into a chamber, which ends in a door. You pound on the door, which opens into a second chamber, and there your road ends. A being sits on a throne, a being with the solemn head of a jackal, holding a staff and an ankh in its crossed arms across its chest.

The chamber is silent. An empty boat rests behind the seated god, and all the walls are painted with scenes that chill your blood . . . for they depict the death and preparation of a body for burial. You're in a funeral chamber! Even the lamps burn low here, and the room is shaded in twilight.

A scroll falls from the lamp of the seated god and rolls across the floor to you. You pick it up and unroll it, thinking that if only you still had the ankh, you might just be able to read it. Maybe it's some sort of magic spell you could use on Set.

You hold it to the light, and the hieroglyphs seem to come to life on their own. Maybe having the ankh on you so long has made the difference, for it is a spell—a spell to awaken the god Anubis, guardian of the gate to the afterworld.

You gulp and lower the scroll and look at the throned being. That has to be Anubis—but who knows if you want him awakened or not? Would he help you against Set?

You cringe as the crash of the outer chamber doors tells you Set has arrived. You grip Sir Hewbert's sword tightly in one hand and the scroll in the other. One way or the other, there's no easy way out of this chamber!

1. *If you use your sword, go to Pathway 33 (page 153).*

2. *If you use the scroll to awaken Anubis, find Pathway 28 (page 133).*

PATHWAY
44

Y ou drop the treasure and dust your hands off. "Not only do the kings and generals of your country go crazy over this stuff, but so do your gods. I think it's all got to be cursed."

Ramses pauses, then looks at you. He nods at last, if reluctantly, and empties his pockets. "You're probably right, Matthew. Besides, if I brought any of this stuff back, they'd probably get me for tomb robbing." He straightens. "What now?"

"We figure out how to get out of here."

You look around the treasure room, and an odd drawing in the corner draws your attention. You go to it, then shout, "Ramses—look at it!"

The shepherd boy joins you, and the two of you look at the drawing. "Is this what I think it is?" you mutter in delight.

Ramses traces it with a forefinger. "It has to be—it's a map of the inside of the pyramid!"

"Then we're right next to an exit. All we have to do is . . ." You twist around on one heel. "Knock out that pillar."

The two of you rush to pull it over, and with a great clanking and grinding, a door opens as the pillar touches the floor horizontally.

You and Ramses grin at each other and rush down the darkened passageway.

The sunlight feels good as the two of you erupt into it, and the last secret door of the pyramid booms shut behind you.

With a screech and a flash of wings, the Sphinx appears from the hills and lands in front of you, licking her chops. Her expression changes as she recognizes the two of you.

"Well . . . that didn't take long," the creature says. "Have you the Beard for me?"

"No," you answer truthfully. "We found it, and other things, and think they're better off lost. All we really found is our friendship for each other. If I'm going to be stuck anywhere, it might as well be right here with a friend like Ramses."

The boy grins and ducks his head as he mutters, "And the same for you, Matthew."

The Sphinx stretches her leonine back and says, "Then I will carry you home, for I owe a favor to you, little master, and that will discharge my obligation to you. No Sphinx likes to remain in the debt of a mortal." She grins suddenly. "Besides, this way, next time I see you I can eat you."

Ramses holds tight around your waist as the two of you mount the winged beast. "I'm really sorry you can't get home," he says, as the beast springs into the air.

"So am I, but—well, I got what I wanted. I wanted glorious adventure, and even though I got it here instead of on the crusades, it's just as good. And I don't want you to feel bad about leaving those gems and jewels behind. I know a little bit about history, and a lot about armor and weapons. I think we're going to do all right!"

THE END

About the Author

RHONDI VILOTT first got hooked on writing in third grade and spent most of her school years working on the school newspaper and in creative writing. She first began working on fantasy and science fiction in the 1970s, and attended the Clarion SF Writer's Workshop in 1979.

Although she has written romances for teens and adults, science fiction is her first love. And, although most writers claim poetic license, Rhondi likes to think she has a pilot's license—for flights of fantasy.

Rhondi lives with her husband, Howard, and their four children in California, and warns all her children's friends that anything they say may be used in a book about them.

Great Science Fiction and Fantasy from SIGNET

**Buy them at your local
bookstore or use coupon
on next page for ordering.**

SIGNET Science Fiction You'll Enjoy

More Science Fiction from SIGNET

Great Science Fiction from SIGNET

(0451)

☐ **INTERGALACTIC EMPIRES: Isaac Asimov's Wonderful Worlds of Science Fiction #1** edited by Isaac Asimov, Martin H. Greenberg and Charles G. Waugh. (126246—$2.95)*

☐ **THE SCIENCE FICTIONAL OLYMPICS: Isaac Asimov's Wonderful World of Science Fiction #2** edited by Isaac Asimov, Martin H. Greenberg and Charles G. Waugh. (129768—$3.50)*

☐ **SUPERMEN: Isaac Asimov's Wonderful World of Science Fiction #3** edited by Isaac Asimov, Martin H. Greenberg and Charles G. Waugh. (132017—$3.50)*

☐ **WIZARDS: Isaac Asimov's Magical Worlds of Fantasy #1** edited by Isaac Asimov, Martin H. Greenberg and Charles G. Waugh. (125428—$3.50)*

☐ **WITCHES: Isaac Asimov's Magical Worlds of Fantasy #2** edited by Isaac Asimov, Martin H. Greenberg and Charles G. Waugh. (128826—$3.95)*

☐ **COSMIC KNIGHTS: Isaac Asimov's Magical Worlds of Fantasy #3** edited by Isaac Asimov, Martin H. Greenberg and Charles G. Waugh. (133420—$3.95)*

☐ **THE SLEEPING DRAGON: Guardians of the Flame #1** by Joel Rosenberg. (125746—$2.95)*

☐ **THE SWORD AND THE CHAIN: Guardians of the Flame #2** by Joel Rosenberg. (128834—$2.95)*

☐ **TIES OF BLOOD AND SILVER** by Joel Rosenberg. (131673—$2.75)*

*Prices slightly higher in Canada.

**Buy them at your local
bookstore or use coupon
on next page for ordering.**

Come Out of This World With SIGNET

"SET! GREAT SET! AVENGE YOURSELF ON THESE INTRUDERS!"

At the priest's cry, you grab your friend Ramses by the arm and start to run, calling to him as you go: "Who is this Set?"

"The most wicked god of all—and powerful! God of darkness and death and destruction!"

The buzz of angry hornets and cruel laughter pursues you through the pyramid's twisting corridors. Finally, you stop by a ramp.

"Is this a way out?" you ask Ramses.

"I hope so, but it could be a trap!"

Suddenly cruel laughter booms, and you spin around to see the corridor blocked by a giant warrior with the head of a demon. You grip your sword as snakes and wicked beasts boil about the evil god's ankles. "We've only got two choices, Ramses. Fight—or take the ramp!"

If you take the ramp, go to Pathway 26 (page 127).

But if you stand and fight, turn to Pathway 13 (page 67).

Whichever choice you make, you will be exploring a new branch along your own private road to the Magic Realms. And no matter how your journey ends, when this adventure is finished, the fun will still go on. Just go back to the beginning of SECRET OF THE SPHINX, and by making different choices, you'll discover a whole new series of exciting and challenge-packed DRAGONTALES adventures.

DRAGONTALES

Choose a Pathway to the Magic Realms

(0451)

#1☐ SWORD DAUGHTER'S QUEST by Rhondi Vilott.
(130820—$1.95)*

#2☐ RUNESWORD! by Rhondi Vilott. (130839—$1.95)*

#3☐ CHALLENGE OF THE PEGASUS GRAIL
by Rhondi Vilott. (130847—$1.95)*

#4☐ THE TOWERS OF REXOR by Rhondi Vilott.
(130855—$1.95)*

#5☐ THE UNICORN CROWN by Rhondi Vilott.
(132025—$2.25)*

#6☐ BLACK DRAGON'S CURSE by Rhondi Vilott.
(132033—$2.25)*

#7☐ SPELLBOUND by Rhondi Vilott. (132858—$2.25)*

#8☐ THE DUNGEONS OF DREGNOR by Rhondi Vilott.
(132866—$2.25)*

*Prices slightly higher in Canada
